NORMAL

Praise for
NORMAL

"Finally! A middle grade book that is brave enough to share a variety of progressive, real-life struggles and circumstances, while also promoting empathy, acceptance, appreciation, and being true to oneself."

—Eevi Jones, Vietnamese-American *USA Today* & *WSJ* best-selling writer and award-winning children's book author

"'Why can't things be normal?' is the cry of this urban tale of diverse young voices, ambitiously and beautifully written yet easy to read, flowing with the secret feelings and hopes of the characters who come alive on the page. The authors have skillfully weaved alternating glimpses of four families in turmoil, all relevant and of this time. *Normal* is also a loving homage to the wonderful Hunter High School on the Upper East Side of New York City."

—Barbara Ames, director of junior and intermediate choruses at Mannes Prep of New School University and former music teacher at Hunter College Elementary School from 1985 - 2002

Even More Praise for NORMAL

"*Normal* is a sparkling and poignant tale of adolescents coming of age in the world's greatest city. Just like the eclectic neighborhoods they hail from, the young protagonists' diverse and compelling exteriors mask complicated homelives and personal struggles. As we learn each character's story, we are reminded of both the beauty and pain of growing up, and the complex challenges that many children are forced to shoulder. A reader will see little bits of themselves in each vignette, whether identifying with the nervousness of attending a new school, finding the courage to share a secret, or the profound ache of losing a parent or watching your hero fall from grace.

"The young people we are introduced to in *Normal* are highly relatable and engrossing and will draw in even the most jaded reader. And in doing so, we realize the moral of this modern, urban fable: that we can relate and connect across differences, even with those who, on the surface at least, seem to share nothing in common with us. The empowering message for readers young and old is (in the words of the great Dr. Seuss), 'Why fit in when you were born to stand out?' Thanks to the authors for the gift that is this special book."

—Saskia Thompson, program director of education at the Carnegie Corporation of New York and former deputy chancellor for the New York City Department of Education

DAVE KERPEN & LINDSAY BROCKINGTON

NORMAL

Dar

Brandylane
Publishers, Inc.
Publishing books since 1985

ISBN: 978-1-953021-63-2
LCCN: 2021953236

Designed by Michael Hardison
Production managed by Mary-Peyton Crook

Printed in the United States of America

Published by
Brandylane Publishers, Inc.
5 S. 1st Street
Richmond, Virginia 23219

 Brandylane
Publishers, Inc.
Publishing books since 1985

brandylanepublishers.com

This book is dedicated to the memory of our fathers,
Peter Kerpen and Jacob M. Brockington, Jr.

1

"Roberta! Roberta!"

That was all David Kaplan could hear his dad screaming as he chased him down their narrow street in Brooklyn, New York.

David's dad yelled his wife's name over and over as he ran. "Roberta, where are you?" he called out, now running onto 6th Avenue, where cars swerved by him on each side, honking their horns as they went by.

Eleven-year-old David ran as fast as he could to catch his dad. "Dad, Mom's at home! Come back home now!" David pleaded. He was more scared than he'd ever been, but he didn't have time to think about it. Cars whizzed by him on the busy avenue block, and drivers shouted as they veered around his dad. David shivered, a bit from the cold but more from the paralyzing fear of his dad getting hit by a car. He summoned up the courage to take a deep breath and try again: "Dad! I need you to listen to me. Come back!"

David caught up to his dad a block and a half away

from their home. They were both out of breath. David held out his hand.

"Okay, son," his dad said and took his son's hand. "You are the son, after all. And I am the father, and Roberta is the holy ghost." David didn't bother asking what he meant.

Together, they moved quickly but carefully to safety, down the avenue block to their home. Dad took a seat on the front stoop of their Brooklyn brownstone, and David sat down beside him.

David breathed a sigh of relief. The smell of the over-flowing garbage can on the sidewalk was rotten, but he was delighted that that was his biggest concern, for the moment at least.

David knew that something was very wrong, but he didn't understand what was going on. It had been a strange few weeks. There was that incident at Hebrew school pick-up, where Dad had said, "Don't forget, Jesus was a Jew." It didn't seem so bad at the time, just odd and out of context. But then it was worse at his bowling league on Saturday morning. It was like Dad was using puns, but taking it to an extreme, bizarre place: "Don't *spare* my feelings, or I'll have to *strike* you. I'll *pin* you to the ground. Just kidding!" He had done it over and over again.

Then, in the middle of dinner that evening, David's dad had stood up and bolted out the front door, screaming for his wife (who had been sitting right next to him at the dinner table). It was really cold out too, and Dad had run outside wearing a t-shirt, shorts, and a pair of old sandals.

David shivered again, pulling his NY Mets jacket tighter around him.

"The child is the father of the man. The child is the father of the man. The child is the father of the man," Dad chanted from their stoop. David sighed and put his hand on his father's back. Both of them had large frames, brown hair, and nearly identical noses and ears; the people walking by on 6th Avenue could immediately tell they were related. They were even wearing matching NY Mets t-shirts, still celebrating the great season that had just ended weeks before. To David, it felt like that had been years ago.

Soon, David's mom burst from the front door and pulled them both into a tight hug. She held her phone in one hand, and her eyes were full of tears. A moment later, a police car and an ambulance showed up, and David watched in stunned silence as the EMTs put his dad in a strait-jacket and shut him in the back of the ambulance. Dad went without much of a fight—he was singing and shouting a bit, but it was more pathetic than agitating at that point. The police seemed kind, but too casual, as if it were a routine operation to assist in tearing families apart.

Once his mom was on the way to the hospital with Dad, David went inside to find his little brother, Philip, and sister, Dani, huddled up in the corner of their shared bedroom, crying. Philip was nine and Dani was six. There were cheerful, colorful posters on the walls, but right now that didn't match the atmosphere in the room at all.

They both ran to David and spoke at the same time.

"What's wrong with Daddy?" Philip asked.

"Is Daddy okay?" Dani asked.

"Daddy's going to be okay now," David reassured them, holding back his own trembling. "I promise."

He had no idea if their dad was going to be okay. But his brother, his sister, and his mom needed him to be strong, to make them feel safe.

David took his siblings down to the basement and set up Minecraft on the Xbox for them. He sat back on the couch next to them, and as Dani and Philip worked on creating their own digital world, David's thoughts wandered. Why did *this* world have to be so crazy? Why did his *dad* have to be crazy? Why did he have to be such a nerd at school? Why did they have to be the only Jewish family in the whole neighborhood? Why couldn't he be like everyone else at school? Why couldn't things at home be calm for even one day?

Why can't things be normal? he wondered.

Why can't I be normal?

2

"Tiffany, grab me another beer, won't you sweetie? This is a big game."

Of course it's a big game, thought eleven-year-old Tiffany as she grabbed a cold Heineken from the refrigerator. *It's always a big game.*

Tiffany, a petite, freckled redhead in pigtails, brought the beer to her dad. He was sitting in his brown armchair in front of the TV, watching a Penn State football game. She sometimes tried to watch the games with him so they could talk, but she couldn't get into sports. Now she just kept him company while she did her homework.

She handed the beer to her dad, who never looked away from the TV. Penn State was winning, so Dad was in a good mood. That was much better than some nights, when his favorite team lost, and Dad yelled at Mom a lot. Sometimes he even yelled at Tiffany, for things that seemed like nothing, like walking in front of the TV.

Mom stayed away from Dad when he was watching games or drinking—or doing both, which was just about every night. That night, Mom was downstairs doing laundry. Or was she upstairs putting it away? Once dinner was over her mother tended to disappear, somehow always out of earshot.

Tiffany's sixteen-year-old sister, Julie, was out with her friends and her boyfriend, Chris—like she was pretty much every night. She was almost never home.

Tiffany sat down on the old beige couch that sat perpendicular to her dad's chair and began working on math homework in her Auburndale, Queens, New York home. It was a pretty nice row-house: it didn't have many windows, but it was spacious by New York City standards. Even though Tiffany and her dad were only six feet apart, it seemed like they were in two totally different worlds.

"Want to check my homework, Dad?" Tiffany asked sweetly, eagerly looking at her father.

Her dad never looked her way. "After the game, hon," he said. "Grab me another beer, would you?" It seemed like she had brought him a beer just five minutes ago, but oh well.

Tiffany had just reached the refrigerator when she heard her dad yelling in the living room. "No! How could you fumble at the three-yard line? They're going to blow this damn game! Unreal!"

The yelling and the change in score worried Tiffany a lot, because she could guess what would happen next.

She was right.

"I'm going out to watch the end of the game at Sully's,"

Dad muttered as he got up off the couch. "This house is giving Penn State bad luck!"

"But, Dad, haven't you had . . ." Tiffany paused. She wanted to remind him he'd had four beers already; that he was drunk, or close to it; that he shouldn't drive; that she was scared, and angry, and sad; that he could watch the end of the game at home and maybe even check her homework like he'd said he would. She wanted to say all those things and more, but he was out the door before she could even finish her sentence.

She sighed and muttered, "Bye, Dad."

Tiffany sat back down on the couch and tried to finish her math homework, but she couldn't focus. She was good at math too—like, straight-A's good—but every time she stared down at her paper that night, she was looking at an ocean of blurry numbers, drifting away without any rhyme or reason.

I'll finish in the morning, she thought. She picked up her iPhone and opened up Snapchat. There, she could escape real life, if only for a little while.

First, Tiffany watched her classmate Mary Buchelli's story. Mary was so pretty, and her family was always together; tonight at a new sushi spot in Astoria.

Next up, Danny Gallo. He and his brothers were watching the football game together.

Angelica DeLuca was out getting her hair done with her older sister, Francesca, who had just gotten a new car.

Fiona Caputo was making cupcakes with her mom for her niece's christening this upcoming weekend.

It was all making Tiffany sick to her stomach. She rubbed her head. *Why is my dad so messed up?* she wondered. *Why is my family so dysfunctional?*

At least on social media she could pretend everything was normal.

Tiffany positioned herself on the lumpy couch to take a selfie with the Penn State game on in the background. But from every angle, you could see beer cans and her dad's empty chair. She got up from the couch and sat on the floor with her back directly in front of the TV. She took a close-up selfie of just her face and the TV playing the game behind her. She typed "#familyfootball" and "#pennstate" for the caption.

She hated football. But all she longed for, more than anything else in the world, was to actually feel normal.

But it wasn't real. Real was her dad driving drunk. Real was her sister out partying. Real was her might-as-well-be blind mom.

Real life was *far* from normal.

3

"Mom, when is Dad picking me up?" Albert asked, sitting anxiously at the kitchen table in their small but cozy Chinatown apartment on a Saturday morning in November. Every minute felt like hours when it was pick-up time.

"I told you. He's supposed to be here at ten o'clock, Albert," snapped his mother. She looked down at her phone as her face strained with anguish.

"Sorry," said Albert. He was a tall, thin, twelve-year-old kid with a pretty bad case of acne. "I'm just so excited—Dad and Guillermo are taking me to Coney Island today!"

"Dad and Guillermo, eh?" said Mom. Her nose had wrinkled up, as though she smelled something bad. "What is that Guillermo up to, anyway?

"Mom, his name is just 'Guillermo,' not 'that Guillermo,'" said Albert, sighing. He was tired of playing this game with his mom. "And he's doing just fine, I think."

"But isn't it weird, Albert? Seeing your father with another man like that?"

Albert had to admit to himself that it *had* been pretty weird. And it was still a little weird. But he didn't want his mom to know he thought that. He figured his mom would take it out on his dad, and then they'd all be worse off.

But yeah, it was weird.

The dad he'd known for all of his life had suddenly become . . . gay. Well, obviously he hadn't suddenly *become* gay out of the blue, but it sure felt that way. One day, after ten years of what seemed like a super normal existence, Albert's dad had sat down with him to tell him the news: Dad was leaving his mom—for a man.

It had seemed so crazy. But now that two years had passed, Albert had gotten used to the whole thing. And he actually liked Guillermo a lot.

Still, it was challenging to navigate between what seemed like two polar opposite worlds, to always do the right thing with the right parent. And Mom didn't make it any easier by not letting him talk about it to anyone, and always asking him about Dad and "that Guillermo". *It's been two years—when is she going to get over it and move on?* Albert thought. A Chinese-American immigrant, Albert's mom was very conservative. So, when his dad had left his mom last year, that would have been enough heartache as it was. But when she found out he left her for another man? That nearly killed her.

When he really thought about it, Albert didn't think his mom would ever get over that.

The doorbell rang.

Albert went toward the door, hoping to leave quickly with his dad and avoid any conflict. His hopes were dashed when his mom skipped ahead of him to get to the door first.

"Well, hello there, Bob," she said as she opened the door. "Long time no talk. How are you? How's . . . *Guillermo?*" she asked, as though it was difficult to spit the word out.

"Hi, Shuchun," Albert's father replied. He was dressed in designer jeans, a soft light blue cashmere turtleneck sweater, and matching blue eyeglasses, and he wore his normally shiny black hair shaved off to peach fuzz.

He smiled at Albert's mother. "I'm fantastic, and Guillermo is just fine too. Thank you for asking. I'm double parked. Can I please take Albert?"

"Just one minute," Albert's mom snapped. "Where's Guillermo? Is he in the car? Maybe he can come out and say hello. *You* sure seem to be good at coming out."

Ouch—there it was. Albert cringed from just behind his mother.

Albert's dad ignored the comment and turned to Albert. "Son, let's go," his dad said. "We have a big day ahead of us in Coney Island. The rides are calling your name!"

This was music to Albert's ears—a day away from his house. He loved his mom, but he needed a space to forget her anger, a space to feel light and happy and . . .

. . . *normal.*

4

"Come here, Alexa," called out her stepmother, Celia—or as Alexa and her best friend, Laura, secretly called her: the Grinch. Alexa was happily studying in her room, but got up and walked into the large, airy kitchen of their Bronx apartment.

Alexa's stepmother was tall and thin, with porcelain skin and long, curly, brown hair, and she was always dressed like she was on her way to some fancy party. "Let me tell you something I want you to never forget, okay?" Celia said as soon as Alexa walked into the kitchen. She took Alexa by the hands. "Just because we're having a low-key Christmas in this household doesn't mean I don't love you. I love you just as much as your mom did, and over time, you'll see that. I just know you will."

Celia's word's took Alexa by surprise and she took her hands back quickly. What was she supposed to do with that? Her father and Celia had met and were married in less than a year, and Alexa could hardly stand the sight of her new stepmother. Alexa just nodded at Celia, turned away, and walked back out of the kitchen.

On the way back to her room, she shut her eyes and slowly rubbed her belly. When she closed her eyes and rubbed her belly, all bad things seemed to drift away, at least for the moment. It was something her mom had taught her.

Alexa was wearing her favorite purple Jimi Hendrix t-shirt that used to be her mother's. It seemed like only yesterday her mom had passed away from breast cancer, even if it was over three years ago. Alexa's eyes were beginning to water, but she tried hard not to let the tears fall. She hurried into her room to catch her breath and compose herself.

Once Alexa was back in the safety of her room, she dug into her pocket for her phone. *The Grinch just told me she loves me as much as my mom*, she texted her best friend, Laura. *WTFFFF!*

"Alexa, are you listening to me?" the Grinch shouted from the kitchen.

"Yup, I hear ya," Alexa shouted back. ". . . you low-key Christmas Grinch," she added under her breath.

Celia was always trying too hard. She wanted them to have cutesy names for each other. She wanted Alexa to call her "S'mom" (short for stepmom), and Alexa wasn't feeling that. She just wanted to call her Celia, and she wanted to be left alone. Alexa only had one mom and that's the way it would always be. Besides, you had to earn the title of

"Stepmother" first. As far as Alexa was concerned, Celia hadn't even come close to earning that title yet.

"Honey, be nice to your stepmother," her father, James, chimed in. He was sitting in the living room, watching Alexa feverishly texting on her phone through her open bedroom door.

Alexa knew her father meant well, and she loved her dad more than anything or anyone in the world, but Celia was so different from her family, especially Alexa's mom. Celia was white, Jewish, and now she was trying to take away Christmas, Alexa's favorite day of the year.

Who does that??? she texted Laura, the only person who would understand.

Grinch, Grinch, Grinch, Laura texted back.

Celia had come out of the kitchen and was now standing at Alexa's bedroom door. "Who in the world are you texting? Who is so much more important than this conversation?" Celia asked, her voice rising with clear annoyance. "I told you, James! You should have never gotten her this phone. The phone becomes their whole life."

Alexa turned her back to Celia. "I'm just texting my friend," she said, and rubbed her belly with one hand, the soft fabric of Jimi's silhouette keeping her calm. With her other hand, she held her phone tight. The only thing worse than the Grinch barking at her about the phone would be if she somehow got her hands on it and unlocked it.

"This phone does me a lot of good, by the way!" Alexa added over her shoulder as she sat down at her desk. "My teachers send us homework on here, and I have study-group chats for every one of my classes."

The Grinch crossed her arms. "Well that's great and all but you're not being nice and I . . ." Celia paused and took a breath. "You can't just . . . walk away or start texting while I'm talking to you." Celia's eyes fell to the floor. "It's rude," she added quietly.

Damn, thought Alexa. What could she say to that? She knew she hadn't been nice, but she wasn't ready for this attention from Celia and she didn't know how to respond to it. She also didn't know how to put that into words, not hurt her stepmonster's feelings, and not get herself in trouble, all at the same time.

Alexa missed her mom so much it physically hurt.

She missed Christmas.

She missed all of the times when things had been *normal*.

She needed to talk to someone.

Without thinking, Alexa unlocked her phone again to text Laura.

In an instant, Celia was reaching for it. "Oh, that's it! I'm taking that phone—" she said, and before Alexa could stop it, Celia had snatched the phone from her hand.

"What's the matter with you?" Alexa screamed. "You're the worst. You're evil! My mother would never rip my phone out of my hand!" She stared at the Grinch as tears started to roll down her face. All she managed to whisper as she clenched her fists was, "You will *never* love me like my mother."

With Alexa's phone in her hand, Celia walked out of the room. Alexa got up, shut her door, slid down the wall, and began to cry.

5

"Catch, nerd herd!" Tony shouted as he threw the basketball toward David and David's red-headed, freckled friend, Gabriel.

David reached for the ball, but he was a split second too late, and the ball jammed his pointer finger.

It was only a week after David's dad had been diagnosed with bipolar disorder, and for David, school was a place to get away from the craziness at home with his family. But some days at school were better than others.

And recess was almost never good.

Mom had insisted he transfer to a fancy private school in Brooklyn Heights this year, as the sixth-grade teacher in his public school was notoriously bad. So David had applied, and thanks to the full scholarship he had received, here he was: in an expensive school with some great teachers . . . and some pretty rotten rich kids.

"I jammed my finger! Damn!" David winced, trying but failing to hold back the pain. Gabriel turned his head away to avoid any eye contact with Tony and his crew.

"Come on, nerd. I just threw you the ball," replied Tony, a large, dimwitted, and popular boy. "Get it together, man."

From across the blacktop, Mr. Schaeffer overheard David and whipped his ahead around. "What's going on here, boys?" he asked.

"Everything's cool, Mr. Schaeffer," Tony reassured him with just a hint of a smirk. "Right, David?"

David's finger hurt really badly. He glanced at his best friend (okay, his only friend) Gabriel and then back at Mr. Schaeffer. He had to make a quick decision.

"Right, Tony." David held his hands behind his back. "It's all cool, Mr. Schaeffer. We're just playing basketball, that's all."

Maybe Tony would respect that David didn't rat him out. Maybe he would even think it was cool of him. David wanted so badly to be cool. He wanted so badly to make friends. But no matter how hard he tried, it never seemed to make a difference—he felt like nobody understood him. So here he was, lying to a teacher, and all he wanted was for things to be normal at school, since they couldn't be normal at home.

But normal seemed impossible.

"Sucker!" said Tony the moment Mr. Schaeffer had walked away. "Dude, that was so funny. The nerd herd is playing ball now!"

David tried hard to hold back tears, but he couldn't do it. It felt like he couldn't escape pain no matter where he went, and he was so tired. He needed help. He needed someone to listen.

Right then, David made a better decision than the one he had just made to not say anything to Mr. Schaeffer: He decided to go see the guidance counselor, Mrs. G.

6

It was 11:58 a.m. on a regular Tuesday, but every day at this time was a big problem for Tiffany.

Lunch was always a nightmare. Basically, Tiffany had two choices: sit by herself and get through lunch as quickly as she could, or try to sit with another group of girls and hope there weren't any problems. Of course, Tiffany would rather not sit alone, but her school was so cliquish, and because she got good grades, Tiffany sometimes felt like she was treated like a freak by pretty much everyone.

12:00. Bell rang. Decision time.

Tiffany slowly packed up her notebook and zipped up her backpack. She was the last one to leave her math class, and she walked slowly through the crowded hallway toward the cafeteria. She didn't want to be the first to sit at a table. That would just set herself up to get rejected by everyone who walked by.

When she arrived, she glanced around the room. It was loud, it was crowded, it was smelly, and it was gross.

She scoped out her options: boys' tables were quickly eliminated; then the cheerleaders. Tiffany continued to scope out the cafeteria. The Spanish-speaking girls; the "artsy" girls . . . Tiffany spotted an empty table. The empty table was tempting, but it would be more embarrassing to sit alone. She gathered up all her courage and picked a different option.

She walked over to the Spanish-speaking girls.

"Este asiento está ocupado," said Julissa, the tallest of the girls, as Tiffany started to pull out the empty chair next to her. Tiffany didn't speak Spanish that well, but she could tell by Julissa's facial expression that she wasn't welcome at the table.

Tiffany's cheeks reddened as she turned around and slowly walked to the artsy table. The artsy girls weren't exactly friendly, but they seemed to be the least cliquish in the whole school. This was her best shot.

Tiffany held her head high and smiled. "Hey girls," she said, "mind if I sit? I just thought—"

But the leader of the artsy pack, Olive—with her serious-looking, deep-set green eyes, crossed arms, and what looked like a million colored bracelets marching up them—interrupted her.

"I don't think so, Tiffany." Olive leaned back in her seat. "We want to relax at lunchtime, not talk about math or whatever it is you nerds talk about every day."

Tiffany's shoulders rose to her ears, and her toes clenched. She opened her eyes wide and tried not to cry. "Okay, then!" she managed to snap at Olive before turning away.

There it was again: the only empty table in the cafeteria. . . .

Tiffany tried to control her breathing and not look sad as she walked over to it, but at least no one would bother her. She sat down in a spot warmed by sunlight spilling through a skylight above. The light reflected the orange in her hair onto the wall and onto her brown paper bag lunch.

Though she didn't look up from the table, she felt like everyone in the whole school was staring at her and laughing.

Tiffany decided two things right then and there:

1. No matter what, she would not cry.
2. She would find a way to get out of this school, one way or the other.

7

It's funny, thought Albert, as he walked from school to his after-school study club. *Just about everyone in my class goes to this study club. They might as well just have it at school.*

There were twenty-five kids in Albert's sixth-grade class, and he saw them just about all day. Sure, he saw students from other grades in the halls, and, of course, they went to gym with another class, but for most of the school day, he saw the same faces.

And here he was walking two blocks in Manhattan's Chinatown to the Preparatory Tutoring Academy's after-school program, which he attended from 3:30 to 6 p.m. every single weekday, with twenty-one out of his twenty-five classmates. It felt to Albert that Chinese parents wouldn't have it any other way. In fact, the only four kids who didn't go to Prep Academy after school were the non-Chinese kids! No matter how much or little your family had, Chinese parents would find a way to fund after-school tutoring classes.

Of course, Albert was used to this. It was really all he'd ever known. But now, in the last two years, he'd had a secret that he was hiding from all of his classmates.

It seemed like every Chinese family he knew was obsessed with good grades, and that every one of those families was perfect. Albert didn't know any other divorced parents, for instance. Nope, Chinese parents figured out a way to stay together, always for the good of the kids and their education. And there certainly couldn't be any gay dads leaving moms for other men! Albert's mom had told him that if that happened, a family would be shunned forever by the entire community.

So, for almost two years, Albert had kept this secret from his classmates. He had almost told his best friend, Paul, twice, but these just weren't things you talk about. He'd be laughed at or shunned for sure. So Albert kept it in. But it was eating away at him.

"Hey, Albert, why aren't you answering me?" asked Paul, who was walking beside him.

"Oh, sorry," replied Albert sheepishly. "I just have stuff on my mind, that's all."

"What kind of stuff?" asked Paul, tapping his finger on his head. "You thinking about today's intro to Hunter?"

"Yeah," Albert fibbed. "I'm nervous but excited!"

Hunter was a school in Manhattan that was thought to be the best school in the city by pretty much every family in Chinatown. It started in seventh grade and went straight through to the twelfth grade, unlike other high schools that started in ninth grade. You had to take a test in the sixth grade to get in, and only the smartest kids in all of New York City would qualify.

If you got in, that meant you'd get six years of the best education in the city—for free. It was like winning the lottery.

Over the past two years, Albert's parents had fought about a lot of stuff. But the one thing they always agreed on was the trajectory of Albert's life: he needed to get good grades, study hard, and get into Hunter.

Today was the day that twenty-two kids in the sixth-grade gifted class at Public School 130 in Chinatown would begin to study for the Hunter test.

Albert and Paul walked down the stairs to the basement-level tutoring center, opened the creaky door to their study room, and saw twenty sets of eyes turn to look at them from around a long wooden table—twenty-one sets if you included their instructor, Mr. Lee. Albert and Paul took their seats quickly.

"Okay, kids," Mr. Lee began, looking around the table, "as promised, today is your introduction to studying for the Hunter test." He smiled. "There are three parts to the test: reading multiple choice, math multiple choice, and an essay. The essay is the most important because it's different from what you're used to studying for."

Albert was trying to pay attention to Mr. Lee, but his mind kept wandering back to his secret. He didn't want to start studying for the most important test of his life with this burden still weighing him down. For the third time in two years, Albert decided he would finally tell Paul. Yeah, that felt good. He would talk to Paul right after this class.

Just then, George, the boy on the other side of Paul, passed Paul a note, and Paul gasped when he read it. Then he turned to Albert.

"Hey, bro," Paul whispered, "this note says your dad is queer. That's not true, is it?"

Albert couldn't respond. *How could this have happened?* he thought. He hadn't told anyone! And now, in the same moment that he had decided to tell Paul, this happened. How was that possible? He could deny it, to be sure. He could lie. But would that do any good? He decided to play dumb.

"What?" Albert shook his head. "What the hell are you talking about, man?"

Paul showed him the note.

"Well, who wrote it?" Albert's voice was getting louder against his will. A little too loud.

"What's the problem here, Albert?" said Mr. Lee, now standing right above them. "Don't you want to know how to construct the perfect essay for the Hunter test? Or should I share with your mother that we're having a problem?"

"No problem, Mr. Lee," replied Albert, lowering his head. "I'll keep quiet now."

Albert kept silent for the rest of the session, but his

mind was racing the whole time. Should he come clean? What would the other kids say? How would they treat him? Would his mom die from shame if she found out? Or do something bad to herself? What about Paul? Would he ever speak to Albert again?

"Albert? Albert! Albert, class is over, man," said Paul, poking Albert hard on the shoulder. "You okay?"

"Yeah, I'm okay," Albert lied. "I'm just fantastic."

8

"So, the square root of 144 is . . . ?"

Alexa looked to her left. No hands in the air. She looked to her right. No hands. She looked behind her. As usual, she was the only student with her hand up. She looked in front of her at Mrs. Kaye, who so desperately seemed to want someone besides Alexa to raise their hand and have something, anything, to say.

But it just wasn't happening.

Alexa only had to wait a few more seconds before Mrs. Kaye called on her.

"Twelve," she said with a sly grin; she knew she was right.

"Thank you, Alexa," replied Mrs. Kaye, nodding. "Correct again." She turned to write the answer on the board, then turned back around to face the class, her bouncy, long, brown ponytail spinning around with her. She fixed her twinkling brown eyes on Alexa. Then she scanned the rest of the room. "At least *somebody* is paying attention."

It's not that the kids aren't listening, thought Alexa. *It's that they don't care as much.* She didn't think it was that none of the other kids were as smart as her, she just thought that maybe she cared more about getting good grades than other kids.

It was because of her mom.

When Alexa had spent her last day with her mom, three years ago, her mom had made her promise two things: that she would always do her best in school and that she would go to college.

Alexa had vowed, from that day forward, to get straight A's, no matter what sacrifices she had to make. It didn't matter if she looked like a big nerd. It didn't matter if she wasn't popular. She knew with each correct answer, her mom was smiling down on her from Heaven.

And then suddenly, Alexa was thinking about Celia. Why was she always in her thoughts? The Grinch wanted to tone down Alexa's family tradition, her connection to her mother. She wanted Alexa and her dad to celebrate Hanukkah. Alexa wasn't Jewish!

Mrs. Kaye interrupted Alexa's thoughts. "Square root of sixty-four?" she begged her students. "Come on now, someone besides Alexa must know this."

Just then, the class was saved by the bell.

"Oh well. It's lunch time." Mrs. Kaye motioned toward the door. "We'll continue with square roots tomorrow."

The kids hurried out of the classroom, but Mrs. Kaye called out again. "Oh, and Alexa, please stay after class for a minute. I need to talk to you."

"Oooh!" teased the class in unison as they hustled out of the room.

Alexa walked up to Mrs. Kaye's disorganized desk. "Am I in trouble?" she asked.

Mrs. Kaye laughed. "No way, young lady!" she said. Her brown skin and bright smile were warm. "On the contrary, my dear. I've been meaning to talk with you about something important." She leaned over, pulled a booklet from her desk drawer, and handed it to Alexa. On the front cover was a picture of a giant castle. "This is Hunter, a special school for the smartest kids in the city, and I think you would love it there."

"I can't afford private school, Mrs. Kaye."

"Well, that's just it, Alexa," Mrs. Kaye said, looking deep in Alexa's eyes. "It's a *public* school. In Manhattan. All you have to do is take a test to get in. With just a little bit more studying, I think you could absolutely get in. It would change your life! With your permission,"—Mrs. Kaye could hardly hold back her ear-to-ear grin—"I'd like to talk to your parents about this."

Alexa's mood immediately went from excitement and interest to frustration. "Thank you, Mrs. Kaye. You can't talk to my parents, but you can talk to my dad if you want to."

Mrs. Kaye's smile dropped. "Of course, Alexa. I'm

so sorry. That's what I meant. I will call your father tonight."

Alexa took a deep breath. "Okay," she said. She was glad Mrs. Kaye understood.

"Oh, and one more thing before you go, Alexa. Really nice job this morning on square roots. Your mother is most certainly looking down at you, proud."

Alexa thought of her mom smiling down on her. She smiled, stood up straight, and walked out of the classroom feeling a bit taller than when she'd walked in.

9

David stood in front of the door to the guidance counselor's office. He lifted his hand to knock, then brought it back down to his side. With a deep breath, he lifted it again and knocked.

"Come on in," said an older woman's voice from behind the door.

David opened the door. Mrs. G had red hair and glasses, and she faced David from behind a big wooden desk. He didn't know much about Mrs. G. He just knew that at orientation, on the first day of school, she had gotten up in front of the whole grade and talked about how any students could come see her anytime they wanted to talk. Something about that speech had made him trust her. David wasn't sure if it was the authentic look in her eyes or her warm smile, but he remembered feeling that she genuinely meant it.

David sat down in a chair across the desk from her.

"David, right?" Mrs. G smiled for a moment, but then her face turned serious, and she folded her hands together on the desk. "What's on your mind today?"

"Well . . ." David sighed, grateful that she had asked. "A lot. There's Tony, he's always giving me a hard time when no teachers are looking."

"That must be really hard," replied Mrs. G.

"Yeah," said David, "but that's just the beginning of it. A lot of the kids are mean. It's like . . . . It's like they're mad at me for being smart or something. I know I'm not a jerk to them—I swear I'm not. I try to be totally nice, actually. But they all treat me like I have a disease just because I get good grades."

"Wow. Have you talked to your parents about this, David?" asked Mrs. G.

That's when David lost it. Tears started streaming down his face.

"They don't care. They have bigger things to worry about. My dad . . . he isn't well. Like, the doctor said there's something wrong with his mind. I don't really know what it all means, but I know it's a real problem. He went to the hospital psych ward a couple of weeks ago. I keep hoping everything's going to be okay, but I don't know anymore."

David muttered the words through his sobs. Mrs. G had moved to crouch at his side as he spoke.

David turned to look at Mrs. G. "I just want things to be normal."

"Normal, huh?" Mrs. G asked. She handed David a tissue and walked back over to sit at her desk. "What does that mean to you?"

"I don't exactly know," David wept. "I want things to be like they used to be: safe. At home *and* at school. I just don't feel very . . . calm." David slowly took a deep breath in to stop sobbing. "I was thinking, Mrs. G . . . maybe I could see a therapist?"

Mrs. G's eyes widened for just a moment, and her head leaned to the side. "Why do you say that?" she asked. "I mean, what would you want to see a therapist for?"

As soon as he had asked that question, David felt like a huge weight had been lifted from his shoulders. "I'd like to talk about my feelings and stuff," he said. "I've been looking online, and it seems like a therapist could help me."

Mrs. G smiled and nodded. "Very well, then," she said. "I'll talk to your parents."

And suddenly, the weight was put back on his shoulders. "They're too busy to care right now, that's part of the problem," David explained. "You see, Dad's sick, and Mom's taking care of him."

"Well, where does that leave you, David?"

"Exactly," he replied, thinking she was finally getting it. "I take care of my little brother and sister, and it's hard."

"Okay, then let me take care of this for you," Mrs. G reassured him. "Oh, and one more thing, David: there's a school that I think you would like. It's a public school, but you have to take a test to get into it."

"Hmm," replied David. "Well, I just started here a few months ago."

"I know," said Mrs. G, flashing her welcoming smile that made David feel immediately at ease. "But I have a good feeling about this. This is a special school, for special young children—like you. Would it be okay if I register you for the test?"

David just wanted to feel normal; he didn't need to feel special. But as he walked out of that guidance counselor's office, he couldn't help but smile.

I guess I could settle for special.

10

This was going to take some courage for Tiffany.

You see, she was used to taking care of things at home—for her dad, her mom, and even her older sister, as strange as that might sound.

But tonight, Tiffany was going to ask for something for herself. She was going to ask her mom for permission to take a test to go to a super selective school called Hunter. Tiffany had done a ton of research. All she needed to do to get in was to pass a test. She was pretty sure she could pass it.

She could already hear her mother's response: "What? Is the neighborhood high school not good enough for you?" or "You want to commute four hours each day? When will you ever be home?"

Tiffany wanted to tell her mother so much: how trapped she felt in her life, how much she hated sitting alone at lunch, how much she hated watching her dad drink so much every night, how her mother was never there when she needed her. She wanted to tell her mom that if no one else was changing anything, well, she just had to try to change things for herself.

Tiffany was sitting at the kitchen counter after school when she heard the front door open and her mom call out, "Tiffany? You home, honey?" Her voice sounded tired.

It was time. Tiffany stood up from the kitchen counter, looked her reflection in the eye on the front of the microwave, took a deep breath, ran her hands down her pigtails, and tightened her fists. *No turning back now*, she thought.

"Yeah, mom," she shouted back as she rushed to the living room. Her mom was already on the couch taking off her shoes, her bag sitting beside her. She had dirty blond highlights that needed a touch-up, a jacket that needed a patch on the elbow, and the faint smell of cigarettes about her that never fully went away.

"I came home right after school and finished my homework already," Tiffany said and smiled, hoping to start the conversation off right.

"That's my girl," Mom replied, but she didn't smile. She got up from the couch and kissed Tiffany on the head, then squeezed her hand without making any eye contact. "Can you please start dinner? I've had a rough day at work, and your father did too."

Very bad sign, thought Tiffany. This meant that her dad was probably already at the bar and might not be home until late. Tiffany felt cheated. This was the one day when she wanted to ask for something; why couldn't today be a good day?

It didn't matter, though. Tiffany felt determined and inspired by the research she had done. Maybe she could use cooking her mom dinner as an opportunity.

"Sure, Mom!" Tiffany said fake-enthusiastically, and she walked to the kitchen.

She prepared her mom's favorite, chicken cacciatore, put it in the oven, whipped up a quick salad, and set the table. She set it for four, but she was pretty sure it was just going to be her and her mom for dinner. When she thought about it, she realized that this situation might actually be working out perfectly.

A few minutes before dinner was ready, Tiffany went upstairs to her parents' bedroom, cracked the door open, and knocked lightly. Mom was still in her work clothes, lying on top of the bed with her eyes closed.

Tiffany whispered, "Hey, Mom, dinner will be ready in ten."

Her mom's eyes fluttered open. "I must have fallen asleep," she said. "I'll be right down, hon."

A few minutes later, with a washed face and a clean pair of sweats on, Tiffany's mom emerged from her bedroom. "Thank you for making dinner tonight, Tiff. It'll just be the two of us. Your father and sister texted me that they won't be home until late," Mom said as she sat down at the dinner table, rubbing her temples. "Man, my head is killing me! There was a terrible pileup on the parkway this morning, and the ER was busier the usual. We got our butts kicked." She paused and looked around at the table, then smiled at Tiffany. "I know I can always count on you around here. The food looks great. And I. Am. Hungry! Will you please pass me the salad?"

This was the perfect moment. It was now or never.

"Don't worry about it!" Tiffany was cheery and upbeat as she passed the salad bowl and sat down next to her. "Hey, Mom?"

"What's up?" Her mom seemed to be concentrating on her lettuce.

"Well, my teachers at school said I should take this test to get into a special school." Tiffany fibbed.

"What school?" Her mom dropped her fork from her mouth and looked at Tiffany, furrowing her brow. "Your current school isn't good enough for you? You do remember I went to that school, right?"

Ugh, so predictable, thought Tiffany. Out loud, she responded more calmly: "It's called Hunter High School. It's a free public school in Manhattan. But you need to take a test to get in."

"I've told you, Tiffany. IS 275 is just fine. That's where I went for middle school, and then Bayside High. You're going to these schools and you're going to do just fine. I never have to worry about you, Tiffany. You're about the only one around here I never have to worry about. Sweetheart, can you pass the salt, please? This chicken cacciatore is great but it definitely needs more salt."

Tiffany was downright mad. How in the world did the conversation go from her asking about this school to her chicken not being salty enough so quickly? And had there been a compliment from her mom in there? It sounded like there was, but she sure didn't feel complimented right about now.

Tiffany wasn't going to give in so easily. "Mom, you're not listening to me. This is important!" she pleaded.

"I sure am listening, dear," said her mom. "I'll tell you what: I'll discuss this school with your father tonight when he gets home from work, and I'll let you know. What's it called again?"

Tiffany slumped back in her chair. "Hunter," she muttered. "Hunter High School."

She felt defeated. She knew that her mom wasn't taking her seriously. She didn't want to have to deal with her drunk dad anymore either, but he was her dad, so she couldn't change that. But those mean girls at school weren't her family, which meant she could change them— and she wouldn't give up until that happened. Tonight just wasn't the night.

"Okay, thanks, Mom," Tiffany sighed, still feeling defeated. "I'm glad you like the chicken."

11

"Come in, Albert. You're early," said Mr. Lee, waving Albert in through the large, old door into the after-school tutoring center.

"Yeah, Mr. Lee. I wanted to chat with you a bit before class today." Albert hoped Mr. Lee couldn't tell that he was out of breath after running ahead of all the other kids for five blocks.

It had been exactly seven days since the rumor came out about Albert's dad, and he felt like seven million people were talking about it. Nobody was talking to *him* about it, but Albert could tell the spotlight was on him.

It was a spotlight he really didn't want.

Mr. Lee put his pen down on the desk. "Okay, Albert," he said, "I think I know what this might be about. Is it that note that got passed around last week?"

Albert paused. That actually wasn't what he had come to talk about, but maybe he *should* talk about the note. He decided to take the easier route: "No. Actually, Mr. Lee, I wanted to talk to you about the Hunter test."

"Oh, okay, Albert," Mr. Lee replied, one eyebrow arched as though he didn't believe him. "Well, you've come to the right place. How can I help you?"

"So, I, um, I'd like to know: how many kids from our school do you think will get in this year?"

"That depends," said Mr. Lee. He looked up at the ceiling, as though remembering. "We usually get eight to ten students in every year. Sometimes more, sometimes less."

"So how about this year, Mr. Lee? Do you think it's a 'less' year or a 'more' year? And how do you like my chances of getting in?"

"I think it's a pretty good year, Albert. Your class is a smart bunch, and you work very hard." Mr. Lee paused, and his brow furrowed. "But why did you rush here to ask all these questions alone?"

Albert thought about why he was asking all these questions: he was determined to get away from as many of these kids as possible and go to a school where nobody (or at least very few people) knew him; he was determined to escape the rumor about his dad—or, actually, the truth about his dad. But with the other kids arriving any second, he couldn't say any of that.

So, Albert instead mustered, "Mr. Lee, I am determined to get into Hunter. I will do everything it takes. Just say it, and I'll do it!"

Mr. Lee looked impressed. "You've got it, young man. I will give you extra studying and homework to do each week. If you are committed, I think you will have a very good chance of getting in. And you will make your parents very proud."

Albert nodded and took his seat as the rest of the study group began to file in.

Very proud, thought Albert. He knew he could make both his mom and his dad proud. Heck, all of his extended family would be proud if he got into Hunter; it was considered the best school by practically everyone he knew. But would it make *him* proud? Would he feel comfortable enough to share the truth about his family there? Or would he still be too embarrassed to share with all those new kids?

Albert didn't know the answers to those questions yet, but he knew he was determined to get into Hunter, and that he wanted to talk to his best friend Paul about everything, sooner or later.

But maybe later.

12

It had been an extraordinary day for Alexa, and it seemed as if it was just going to keep getting better. The Grinch was coming home late from work, so Alexa would get to have dinner alone with her dad. That was Alexa's favorite time at home by far. She put on her lucky Jimi Hendrix t-shirt again. She wore it a lot, but it always calmed her. If Mrs. Kaye was going to call about Hunter, she could use the extra luck.

She was surprised that Mrs. Kaye hadn't called yet, but she figured her math teacher had just been busy. Besides, even though she liked Mrs. Kaye a lot, she knew she was kind of flaky. Maybe she'd forgotten completely.

"Dad, what's for dinner?" she called from her room. Alexa wasn't sure if it would be an order-in night or maybe a Dad's famous grilled cheese night. She had to admit that the one nice thing about the Grinch was that, since she had come around, Dad had been cooking again.

"I don't know, hon," her father called back from the

living room. "Maybe we should order in. How would you like Chinese food?"

"Yes, yes, yes!" replied Alexa. She ran out from her room and gave her dad a big hug. They had just finished the hug when Dad's phone rang.

"Hello?" said Dad. "Oh, hi, Mrs. Kaye! Is everything alright?"

It was Mrs. Kaye calling! Alexa was so excited, but she could only hear half of the conversation. She frowned as she listened to her father say, "I see," and "Interesting," and "Really?" over and over again.

It sounded promising, though! That is, until the end of the conversation, which Alexa heard crystal-clear: "Okay, great. Thanks again for calling. I'll talk to my wife and get back to you."

Talk to my wife? Alexa screamed inside of herself. *Did he really just say that? No, no, he couldn't have. The Grinch is not going to decide my future*, she thought.

Dad hung up the phone and turned to Alexa. "That was a really interesting call from your math teacher, hon. Let's talk about it when the chicken with broccoli gets here." He winked at Alexa. "And you can even hold the broccoli tonight."

The next thirty minutes felt like thirty hours. Alexa texted with Laura and read DC Comics until the doorbell rang and the Chinese food arrived.

"Okay, so," Dad finally began, once they had each filled up a plate with food and sat down to eat. "Mrs. Kaye called about this school that she thinks you should take a test for. It's called Hunter and it's in Manhattan, on the Upper East side." Dad paused for a moment and bit into his favorite: orange chicken.

Alexa put her fork down. "Sounds really cool," she said. "Do you think I could get in?" She was excited to be talking about this before her dad talked to the Grinch about it.

"I do, I really do," Dad responded. "I think you can do just about anything you set your mind to, and this is no different."

"Okay, I'm in," said Alexa. "This is going to be great!"

"Well, there's one concern I wanted to talk to you about, Alexa." Her dad never called her Alexa unless she was in trouble. It was always nicknames like "hon" or "Lex Luther" (her dad was a big Superman fan) or "Al" for short. "Mrs. Kaye is concerned about you being one of only a few Black kids in the whole school, and you know I think it's important for you to be around other Black kids . . . kids like *you*. Celia is less concerned than I am about this, but we should still talk about it when she gets home."

"*What*? You talked to her about this already?!" Alexa was angry and confused. She hadn't heard him on the phone with the Grinch after Mrs. Kaye called. Even more confusing: why was the Grinch taking her side? Alexa didn't understand.

"I texted her while we were waiting on the Chinese food. Alexa, she's my wife. I have to talk to her about these things," Dad argued. "And you know, I'm not the only one who thinks it's important for you to be surrounded by other people of color. Your mom would have wanted that too."

That made Alexa pause. "How do you know there won't be other Black kids at Hunter?" she asked.

"Mrs. Kaye mentioned it. And I'm not saying that there won't be any Black kids and you'll be in some crazy alternate universe. I'm just saying that it will be very different from what you've been used to up until now." Dad smiled and looked Alexa deep in her eyes. "I'll tell you what," he added. "If this is that important to you, you can take the test and then I guess we can figure the rest out later."

"Thank you, Dad!" Alexa squealed in delight. "You won't regret this. I'm going to get in, and I'm going to get good grades there, and I'm going to go to the best college!"

Her dad looked at her with a proud gleam in his eye. She knew he loved her so much, even if he *was* delusional about the Grinch.

Alexa lifted her Coke can toward her dad. "For Mom!"

"Very well then, Alexa." Her dad smiled, tapping her Coke with his. "For Mom."

13

"David, I got the strangest call today," Mom said as David sat down to have his after-school snack of two double chocolate chip cookies and almond milk (for health).

"Oh, yeah?" asked David, biting into his cookie and playing dumb. "What was it about?"

"Well, your guidance counselor called, and she said the most remarkable thing: that you had actually gone to her and told her you wanted to try therapy."

David put down his cookie and swallowed. He looked up. "Well, yeah, Mom," he said. "It's just that, with Dad getting sick and all, and bullies at school, well, I just wanted someone to talk to, that's all. I hope you're not mad at me."

"Mad?" His mom looked offended. "No, I'm not mad. I'm touched. Surprised. Proud. No, I'm not mad. I realize with everything that's going on, I haven't had a lot of time for you lately." She sighed. "So, if you want to go to a therapist, I'd be happy to support that. Wait, bullies? Did you say bullies at school?"

That was all a lot for David to unpack. But he started by answering her last question first.

"Yeah, I didn't want to tell you, because you have more important things to worry about, like Dad. But . . . some kids at school have been giving me a hard time, especially at recess. I'm sorry, Mom."

Now Mom definitely looked mad. Her brow raised, and she threw her hands up in the air. "Sorry?!" she exclaimed. "You don't have to be sorry! I'm the one who should be sorry. Bullies! I can't believe it. I moved you to this new school, and it's a complete disaster. I'm so sorry, David." She put her head in her hands.

"It's okay, Mom," David replied, shifting from side to side. "I don't want you to be upset. I just want to maybe see a therapist, if that's okay?"

She looked up at him. "Of course it's okay. I'll make it happen right away. I know someone, a friend of a friend. And another thing: your guidance counselor mentioned this school—"

"Hunter!" David interrupted. "Yeah, I looked it up online on the way home. It sounds really cool. They call me a nerd at school. Hunter looks like a dream come true for nerds! Can I go there?"

"It sounds like a hard test. I don't want you to be too disappointed if you don't get in, kid," Mom said. "But if you can, yes, you can go there. You're the smartest kid I know!"

David was relieved. He couldn't have imagined a better

outcome from visiting the guidance counselor if he tried. He felt brave. He felt proud. He felt . . .

"Oh, and one more thing, David," said Mom, her smile melting into a frown. "Some bad news, actually. Your father isn't doing too well on the current meds that he's on. I think he's going to check himself back into the hospital tomorrow. I wanted to prepare you, as I may have you and your brother and sister stay with the Johnsons for a bit while I deal with this."

Well, that sucks! thought David. Just when things seemed to be looking up, his mom had to go and drop a horrible bomb like that. *Why can't we be a normal family for two seconds?*

David felt sad. He felt guilty for being selfish. He felt out of control. He felt far from normal.

He tried to focus on the plus side: he was going to get to see a therapist. That could be a fun adventure. And speaking of adventures, this Hunter school sounded pretty awesome.

14

When Tiffany's dad wasn't drunk, he was her favorite person in the world. Kind. Charming. Funny.

Since talking to her mom about Hunter didn't work, Tiffany had a new plan: talk to her dad and convince him to let her take the test. She just had to figure out how to get to him when he was sober. She knew he drank the least on Tuesday nights ("Tame Tuesdays," she called them), whether it was because it was the only night of the week when the entire family was usually under one roof, or maybe it was just her dad's day to take a break, she didn't know for sure. She definitely knew she couldn't ask on a football or a weekend night. If she played her cards right, and everything fell into place exactly so, she would have her chance.

She planned to ask him that next Tuesday, after dinner but before he passed out on the couch, during what would likely be a two-hour window.

When Tuesday finally arrived, Mom had had a good day. Such a good day, in fact, that she made Dad's favorite for dinner: steak. This was a good sign. Dinner was great because all four of them were actually at the dinner table. It was also great because it was, thankfully, uneventful. Tiffany and her parents and sister had a calm, nice, normal meal with normal conversation.

Dad had two bottles of Guinness at dinner, but that was no big deal. Then he went to the recliner to settle in for the night and watch reruns of *Law & Order*, his favorite show. As long as her sister and mom went upstairs, she could hatch her plan.

A few minutes later, Tiffany's sister was out the door to meet her boyfriend to "study." A little while after that, her mom said she needed a bath, and upstairs she went.

Tiffany couldn't have planned it better herself.

Once the coast was clear, she went to the fridge, grabbed a Guinness, opened it up, and walked it over to the recliner.

"Want a cold Guinness, Dad?" she asked with a smile.

"You read my mind, Tiff!" replied her dad with a big smile. "Thanks, hon. Why don't you grab a seat and watch some cops and robbers with your old man? Or do you have too much homework tonight to hang out with me?"

Tiffany quickly sat on the end of the couch closest to his recliner. "I think I can watch, Dad." she smiled coyly. Everything was going perfectly. She nodded at the screen. "I can't believe how much you love this old show."

"It's mostly nostalgia, kiddo. And some decent story lines. Plus, they don't have the horses on TV. I've got some good money on Cotton Tail in the third race tonight, but I'll have to watch my phone for updates on that." He looked down and checked his phone. "It's a long shot, but you never know, right?"

That was her opening! "Right!" said Tiffany. "Speaking of a long shot . . ."

"Oh, boy," interrupted Dad as he turned toward Tiffany, the smile no longer on his face. "What do you want? I should have known when you brought me that Guinness. What is it and what is it going to cost me? I'm not made of money, you know. This house doesn't pay for itself!"

Tiffany was stunned. She couldn't believe how worked up Dad had gotten so quickly, but she couldn't give up before she even tried. She had to calm the situation down.

"Well, Dad, first of all, what I'm asking for is totally *free!*"

"Yeah, right," he replied as he guzzled down the rest of his beer. "Nothing in life is free. What is it already?"

Tiffany gulped, but she sat up straight. "Well, I'm not happy going to school where I'm at now, and I found a school in Manhattan that I really like. It's called Hunter. And it's free. And the only thing I have to do to get in is take a test and, well—"

"I bet your mom already said no, right?" Dad interrupted. "Because I'm sure she did. She went to Bayside High, and you're going to go to Bayside High. I'm pretty sure that's about how it went, isn't it?"

Tiffany just stared at her father, unable to respond.

"I've known your mother a long time, you know, Tiff," he continued. "And I know her well enough to know she'll have my head if I say anything to her." He took another sip of beer and looked back toward the TV.

Tiffany slumped back into the couch and looked down at her lap, trying to fight the tears from coming.

"But . . ." she heard her dad say. She looked up to see him looking at her again. "I'll tell you what," he said, "I'll talk to her, and I will look at this Hunter school online and . . ." He sighed. ". . . I'll see what I can do."

Tiffany flew to him and put her arms around him. "Thank you so much, Daddy!" she shouted. "I love you so much!"

"All right, all right, easy there. I haven't done anything for you yet, Tiff." He returned the hug and pulled on her braid. He smelled like beer, but she didn't care. "Now do me a favor and grab me one more cold one. Jack McCoy is about to do his cross examination."

Tiffany skipped out of the room and grabbed her dad another Guinness. As she headed to her own room after the nightly news was over, she felt like her life was taking a turn for the better.

15

It was 10:45 p.m., and Albert's mom still wasn't home. She often got home a little late, but never past nine. He knew how important it was to her to be home to help with his homework.

Albert was worried. Mom already worked hard in a factory not too far from their apartment. She was always working Monday through Saturday, and then Sunday was church, and then it was back to work the next day. When did she have time for fun?

She worked that hard just so Albert could have everything she didn't have as a kid. She sacrificed everything so that he could succeed in school and in life. Albert was going to work super hard to get into Hunter, and he was going to make her proud. He just had to.

He also knew she would be crushed if he told anyone their family secret. He didn't want to disappoint her, but it was just so . . . hard.

Albert had been planning on talking to her about it tonight when she got home from work, but now it was

10:48 p.m., and there was still no sign of Mom.

At 11:02 p.m., he heard her keys in the lock. "Hello, Albert!" she called as she came through the door. Her voice sounded excited, but Albert saw the bags under her eyes.

"Hi, Mom!" said Albert from his seat at the kitchen table. "How was your day?"

She walked into the kitchen and kissed his head. "Good," she replied. "Well, a little long. Did you eat dinner? I left pork buns in the refrigerator for you." She reached into the refrigerator, took out some leftover soup, and put it in the microwave.

"Yup. No worries, Mom. Sit down. Relax. I have something exciting to tell you."

"Great!" Mom sighed with relief as she sat next to Albert. "Get any tests or quizzes back from school today?"

"Nope, but I had a conversation with Mr. Lee after school. He thinks I have a really good shot at getting into Hunter based on my practice tests."

"Hush, son!" she blurted. "You know you will jinx it if you say that!"

"Sorry, Mom," Albert said, "but—"

"But nothing," she interrupted. "You know better than that. I am glad you are doing well, but now is not the time to be boastful. You must continue to work hard and be humble." She walked with purpose to the microwave, took out the soup, and brought it to the table.

"I know," said Albert. "I'm sorry." He should have

remembered how superstitious his mom was about these sorts of things. He had just wanted to share the good feedback from Mr. Lee. Like he wanted to share how he was feeling about the secret.

"Mom," said Albert, looking down at his hands, "there's something else."

"What is it, son?" asked Mom, sipping her sweet and sour soup.

Albert took a deep breath and then said everything very fast. "It's hard not being able to talk to anyone about Dad. I know you're really embarrassed and everything, but I was wondering if you would be okay with me talking to Paul about it. I know he wouldn't tell anyone."

Mom looked up from her soup but remained silent. After a moment, she simply shook her head, and then went back to the soup, as if nothing had happened.

"Mom?" Albert said desperately.

Mom looked up again from her soup, then back down, then back up again. Finally, she spoke. "This conversation is over. Your father has brought shame upon our family. You can bring us back our respect. Now focus your energy on the Hunter test, not on your father."

Albert knew his mom well enough to know that the conversation was, in fact, over. "Okay, Mom." Albert stood up from the table. "I'm going to go to my room and study."

He went right to his room, but studying wasn't the first thing on his mind. Instead, he pulled out his phone and texted Paul, *FT? Something big to tell you.*

As soon as Paul replied, Albert was going to FaceTime him and spill it, once and for all.

16

Alexa was excited. She couldn't believe how things were going her way lately! Her teachers at school were being extra helpful (especially Mrs. Kaye), and the kids weren't even a bother to her. It's not that they had changed, but now she let it go because she knew she was working hard to get into Hunter and make her mom proud.

After school, she bounded into her apartment and shouted for her dad. "Guess what!" she called. "I got a ninety-nine on my math test! The whole class got in the seventies, and I got a ninety-nine!"

She hung her backpack on the coat rack and looked in the living room and the kitchen, but it seemed like her dad wasn't home.

"Ninety-nine?" the Grinch said as she came out of her bedroom. "Not bad!"

"Oh. Hi, Celia," replied Alexa.

"If you can get a ninety-nine, you can get a hundred!" Celia said and laughed.

Alexa stopped and stared at Celia. "Are you kidding

me?" Alexa shot back. She wondered how it was humanly possible for her to go from being excited to annoyed so quickly.

"Well, no. I mean, yes. I am kidding," Celia stammered. "It's something my father used to always say when I almost got a hundred on a test."

I wish she wouldn't try so hard, Alexa thought, then answered Celia out loud, "Well it wasn't very funny. I did the best in my class, like I always do. I'll try and get that hundred percent next time." Alexa flared her nostrils and rolled her eyes.

Alexa went to the junk drawer by the front door, grabbed her phone that she wasn't allowed to take to school anymore, and headed to her room. She texted Laura, who she was sure would appreciate her score of ninety-nine. Laura was her best friend, and the thought of not going to the same school as her was the worst.

Guess what! she texted. *I got a ninety-nine on my math test!*

Niiiiiice! Laura replied.

Thanks! Alexa texted. *You have to take the Hunter test with me.*

I might take it but I'm not getting in. It's soooooo hard.

Alexa frowned at her phone. *How do you know? You might get in!*

I'm not getting in.

I'm getting in!

Yeah, but your so smart!

You're, Alexa corrected her. She knew that a lot of people made that mistake, but her mom had taught her not to make it, so she didn't.

Oh. Sorry, texted Laura. *See? Lol. You're smarter than me!*

You're smart too! GTG.

Alexa wasn't sure Laura would get into Hunter. And she wasn't sure she'd ever like the Grinch. But she was sure she was going to keep working hard, keep getting ninety-nines, and get into the top school in the city.

17

It had seemed like such a good idea to David at the time: somebody there just to listen to him, somebody to tell him everything's going to be okay, somebody to help him feel more normal.

But now that going to see a therapist was a reality, David was getting nervous.

He wasn't nervous about the physical "going" part. David had been as independent as just about any eleven-year-old in Brooklyn over the past six months, taking the B63 public bus to and from school on his own while the rest of his private-school classmates took the school bus or were dropped off in fancy cars or Ubers.

No, "going" wasn't the part that made him nervous. As David got off of the F train he had taken after school and began to walk the two blocks to his new therapist's office, he thought about what would happen when he got there, and that scared the heck out of him. What if he didn't like Dr. Tirolo, the friend-of-a-friend therapist his mom had selected for him? What if he didn't feel comfortable talking? What if she didn't tell him everything was going to be okay? What if everything *wasn't* going to be okay?

With his dad still in the hospital, Tony and the other bullies at school getting worse every day, and his mom too busy to help him, well . . . with all of that, how could it ever be okay?

David arrived at 236 7th Street: Dr. Mary Tirolo's office. He looked up at the tall, black door and swallowed. Then he rang the downstairs bell.

After what seemed like forever, an older lady opened the door. David wasn't sure at first how old she was, but the gray hair and soft lines at the corners of her eyes gave him a hint.

"Oh, hello! You must be David. Come in!"

She seemed nice enough. David walked into the basement office and took a seat on a small, comfortable couch. Or maybe it was a super large chair. He looked around. The small office was cluttered, with stacks of books and papers everywhere. There was a grandfather clock in the corner of the room, which looked way too big in such a small office.

Dr. Tirolo sat down in a chair facing David. "So, your mom told me the story of how you went to the guidance counselor to ask for therapy. How brave!"

Okay, he liked her already. "Well, Dr. Tir . . . Dr. Tiro . . ."

"You can call me Mary," she said, smiling. "It's much easier."

"Well, Dr.—I mean, Mary, I guess I've just heard family members and friends of the family talk about therapy in the past," David said humbly, even if he was feeling very proud in that moment. "I figured I could talk about stuff, you know."

"Well, I do know," she replied. "That's pretty much how this works. You talk about stuff, and I listen. So, tell me what's going on with you right now."

It was an invitation David sorely needed. "Well, my dad is going crazy, like for real, and I get bullied at school, and I have to take care of my brother and sister, and I'm in the nerd herd, and my aunt died, and I hate school, and . . ." David realized he was out of breath. He paused, took a deep breath, and blinked to stop the tears that were begging to come out. "And I just . . . I wish my family could be normal and school could be normal, and well, I wish *I* were normal."

The room was quiet for a moment. "Wow," said Mary. "That sounds like an awful lot to deal with."

David couldn't hold the tears back anymore.

He unloaded more tears than he remembered ever crying before. It was like all of the emotions stored up inside of him released all at once, like a river bursting through a dam.

"I just . . . I can't, I . . ." David tried to talk through the tears, but his breath kept catching, and it was no good.

"I understand," said Mary, "and it's all right to cry. Let it all out."

Oddly enough, as soon as Mary said that, David felt better; his breathing slowed, and his tears all but stopped. He only remembered having cried a handful of times over the past five years, but each time, he could remember his parents telling him, "Don't cry."

Through the last bit of sniffles, he continued to talk—and talk, and talk, and talk—about his parents, his dad being sick, about missing his old school and hating the school he was at now, and wanting things to be normal. He didn't let Mary get in another word for what felt like hours but must have actually been the forty-five minutes the therapy session had been scheduled for.

"David," Mary said softly, "I'm afraid it's just about time for us to stop. I have another client coming to see me in a few minutes. But I have some homework for you, something to think about."

"Homework?" David asked. Up until now, despite all the crying, he had been feeling pretty good. But he didn't want any homework.

Mary laughed. "It's not so bad, I promise," she said. "I heard you mention a couple of times that you wished your family was 'normal,' and that your life was more 'normal.' For next week, I'd like you to think specifically about what a normal life would look like for you."

"So, like, describe a normal family? That's easy!" said David, chuckling.

"Okay then. I look forward to seeing you again next week, David," Mary said as she stood up from her chair.

"Thank you for giving this a shot. You really are a brave and special young man."

David still didn't feel normal, but hearing that, he sure did feel pretty good.

18

It had been six days since Tiffany had talked to her dad about letting her take the test to go to Hunter. Six days, and she still hadn't heard a thing from either of her parents. Sure, she'd been busy with stuff after school, and her mom had some work things, and her dad had been out late at the bar most nights, but still. . . . Where was her answer?

So, she did what anyone her age would do when she needed an answer from an adult right away: she texted them. Friday after school it took her almost twenty minutes to write and proofread the perfect text before she sent it: *Mom, Dad, I know you've been super busy, but the deadline to submit paperwork to take the Hunter test is in one week, so I kinda need to know now if I can take it. I promise to do extra chores around the house if you let me take it. Thank you for being the best parents ever. [Heart emoji], T*

Then she waited. Neither of her parents were tech-savvy enough to turn off read-receipts, so she could see that they both read the text almost as soon as they got it; yet fifteen minutes later, there was still no reply. Tiffany decided to listen to music to make the time go by faster. She put on Joe Jonas and opened Instagram to distract herself.

Everyone else's lives were perfect. Except hers. *Like, like, like.* She liked all the pretty pictures of her classmates and the cool places they were going. Why didn't her family go to cool places? More importantly, why couldn't they even get back to her about taking a test to go to the *best* school in the city? All she could think was that it shouldn't be this difficult.

Okay, now she was getting angry. She was just about to send another text when she got one from her dad: *We'll talk about it tonight, T. Busy day at work.*

Tiffany stared at the text. That seemed promising, actually. No reply from Mom yet, but her dad had said they'd talk about it that night.

Thanks! [Heart emoji] x3, Tiffany wrote back. Then, she planned: she would make a delicious dinner for her parents to get them ready for the big answer. It was Friday night, so her sister would be out late with her boyfriend. She would make her dad's favorite. No, better yet, she'd make her *mom's* favorite again: chicken cacciatore. And this time, she'd make it perfectly.

Tiffany made sure she had all the ingredients in the house. At 6 p.m. she preheated the oven and began cooking what would be her best meal ever. While the chicken was cooking, she set the table with the fancy dinnerware they only used for special occasions. She knew her mom might get mad about that, but she figured as long as she promised to do all the dishes, she couldn't possibly be mad.

Everything came out looking great. It was seven o'clock, so her parents would be getting home soon. Tiffany sat at the kitchen table, anxious but excited.

Mom came in at 7:10. "Whoa, somebody thinks today is special enough for a fancy dinner, huh?" Mom teased as she walked in.

"Well, Mom, I—"

"I'll be down soon," Mom interrupted. "Just need to change, hon." She started up the stairs. "What did you make for dinner?"

"Chicken cacciatore!" Tiffany called to her.

"Nice!" said Mom. "My favorite."

Mom shut the door to her room to change, and Tiffany waited for her dad to get home. Then, everything would be perfect.

After school, she had turned her phone volume way up so she could know right away when her parents responded to her text. But since her dad had barely responded, the silence of her phone was deafening. All she wanted was confirmation that her dad was on the way home.

At 7:26, he texted the family chat: *On my way home for dinner. Long day, going to stop by Sully's for one drink. Won't be long.*

Tiffany gulped. Sully's was her dad's favorite bar. She'd seen this before. His text might mean: "One drink. Won't be long," but it might also end up meaning: "Drinking all night. Won't be home until you're asleep."

This was not good news. She could keep dinner warm for a while, but could she keep her mom happy enough to give her the answer she wanted when her dad got home?

Her mom had obviously seen the text too. "We're eating by eight, Tiff," she called down the stairs. "I'm not letting that chicken cacciatore get cold!"

Tiffany knew it was unlikely her dad would get home by then. This was starting to feel like an epic disaster.

7:30 rolled around. No dad, no text.

7:45. Still no dad, no text.

Tiffany could feel her chances of going to Hunter slipping away with each minute. She took a chance and texted her father solo: *Hey Dad, what time are you going to be home? Mom really wants to have dinner soon.*

No reply.

8:00. Still no reply.

8:15. Still no reply.

At 8:20, Mom patted Tiffany on the shoulder. "Come on, Tiffany. Let's not waste a delicious dinner. Dad can have leftovers when he gets home."

"Okay, Mom." Tiffany hung her head, but tried not to sound as disappointed as she felt.

The two of them ate, talking about everything . . . and also nothing. Tiffany knew better than to bring up her dad or the Hunter test—things simply weren't done like that in her family. Her mom loved the meal, so that was good. But when they finished up at nine, and there was still no sign of her father, Tiffany had to admit that she wasn't going to get any good news that night.

"Thank you, Tiffany. This meal was delicious. Your father will be sad he missed it. Do ya mind doing the dishes?" Mom seemed genuinely appreciative, but clearly disappointed in Dad too.

"Sure, Mom. No problem," said Tiffany. "You go upstairs to rest. I got this."

"You're the best, Tiff," said Mom. "And I'm sure we can talk about things with your father soon." She yawned. "I have got to get some sleep. Goodnight!"

And with that, her mom's night was done, and so were Tiffany's chances of getting the thumbs up from both of her parents that night.

But Tiffany wasn't going to let her dad get away with dissing her so easily. She decided to wait up for him on the couch. She'd just scroll through Instagram and TikTok until he got home.

10:00. Nothing.

11:00. Nothing.

By 11:30, Tiffany wasn't sure she could stay up much longer, but she had to try. She pulled up Instagram again and clicked on a story from her cousin in Florida . . .

"Honey, what are you doing on the couch?" Dad tapped Tiffany on the shoulder to wake her up.

"Dad?" Tiffany sat up and rubbed her eyes. "What time is it? I made you dinner!"

"It's a little after one. I got held up, and my phone died. Sorry about that. I'll make it up to you, kiddo."

Tiffany glanced up at her father and then down at her phone. 1:46 a.m.

She smelled his breath and sighed.

"Goodnight, Dad," she said quietly. Tiffany was tired. Her legs and arms felt like they weighed a million pounds. Her chest felt like a ship had sunken in its center. Her mind was fogged, and she could feel her pulse racing around her head. Tiffany walked up to her room and fell down onto her bed. She was glad she was so tired that her disappointment wouldn't keep her awake. And it didn't.

19

Albert stared at the time on his iPhone as he waited anxiously for Paul to text him back. It was 11:18, but Albert knew his friend wasn't asleep. He was always up late studying and listening to music.

One minute had gone by since Albert had asked Paul to FaceTime. Then two more minutes, then three. Finally, Albert got a reply to his text: *Sure. Give me 2 min.*

Albert had two minutes until he would either tell Paul the secret about his father or chicken out, and no matter how many times he weighed the pros and cons, he still couldn't decide. On the one hand, the secret was really weighing on him. On the other hand, his mom had clearly told him not to say anything. Paul was his best friend, and if Albert finally told him, he might be able to concentrate better on school and studying for the Hunter test. But what if Paul abandoned him once he told him the truth?

The phone lit up with a FaceTime call. He had to decide. Quickly.

"Yo, dude. What's up?" Albert answered, trying to look calm but clenching his teeth.

"You tell me, brother," Paul replied casually, shrugging with his hands turned up. "You're the one who said he had something big to tell me!"

Albert paused. He'd known Paul for so long. He knew he could trust him. Why was this so difficult? He wondered whether his heart was beating so loud that Paul could hear it across phones.

"Come on, man, out with it!" Paul laughed. Something about that laugh—kind, and not even a bit judgmental—was all Albert needed.

Albert took a breath, straightened up, and blurted it out: "It's true about my dad. He left my mom. I mean you knew that part already. But the thing is . . . he left my mom for a dude. Yup, my dad is gay. There, I said it."

As soon as Albert said it, he felt a rush of emotions. First, he breathed a huge sigh of relief; at long last, the secret was out! But that relief was quickly replaced by fear; what did Paul think? Paul's face was impossible to read. And then that fear turned to dread, and Albert looked away from the screen as he realized there was no way—

"Bro. Of course your dad's gay, man," Paul said. Albert turned his head back to the screen. Paul appeared nonchalant as ever and lifted his arms as if to give Albert a hug across phone screens. "I knew that," Paul continued. "Was kind of obvious. My cousin's gay. So what?"

Albert felt like an enormous boulder had been lifted off his shoulders. He laughed at nothing in particular. He felt like he was so light, he could float. It took him another moment to fully register what Paul had said. "Wait, your cousin's gay?" Albert asked. "Which one? I didn't know that."

Paul laughed again. "I didn't tell you, dude. Same reason people can't know about your gay dad. We're Chinese! We don't talk about this stuff." Albert just stared at Paul, so Paul continued. "So, it's cool that you told me and all, but we don't have to talk about this again. And you shouldn't tell people—at least until you're old or something."

Whoa, Albert thought. That was a lot to digest. Paul was the friend who always told it like it was, and what he said made a lot of sense. But he was supposed to feel better having shared this secret, and instead he felt worse, as if more pressure had built up inside of him and was still waiting to explode.

"Okay," Albert finally said out loud. "Like, I can't talk to anyone about this?"

"Dude, let me repeat myself: We are Chinese. Your mom is, like, first-generation immigrant Chinese. This is no joke." He paused, and then sighed before he continued. "Look, if you want to talk to me about it again, that's cool. You know I'll always be there for you, man. But I'm telling you, don't risk your whole reputation in Chinatown over one stupid thing. Don't tell anyone else. Like, ever."

Albert was bummed, but he didn't want to ruin his reputation in Chinatown or with his mom.

"You're right, man," Albert said. "Thanks for always telling it to me straight."

"Hahaha! Straight is right!" replied Paul.

Albert tried to laugh, but he couldn't. "Later, man."

"Later."

Albert hung up the phone. Sure, he felt better having finally shared his secret. It felt good to know he wasn't alone—heck, even Paul had a family member who was gay.

But not telling anyone else, ever again?

Maybe it would be okay, Albert reasoned, as long as both he and Paul got into Hunter.

For the first time in a long time, as soon as his head hit the pillow, Albert fell right asleep.

20

The plan to get into Hunter was working pretty well for Alexa—she was getting good grades, keeping her dad happy, and staying generally upbeat—except at school, that was.

It felt like the better she did at school, and the harder she studied, the less other kids liked her. Laura had gone from her best friend to her only friend. At first, Alexa was so focused on her goal that it didn't bother her. But soon, the loneliness crept up, and she couldn't help but hear the whispers as she walked by.

The main problem was Natasha and her group. Natasha was an outright bully. Alexa's father had explained to her that bullies often had low self-esteem and felt like they had to put others down in order to feel better about themselves. Whatever the reason, Natasha was very good at bullying, and Alexa was on the receiving end. It didn't help to think about Natasha's low self-esteem when Alexa was the one being put down.

Natasha rarely talked to Alexa—she mostly just

snickered at her—but when she did, she always had something nasty to say. She called her "nerd" or "angel" or "loser." The names changed, but the nastiness remained the same.

At the end of a cold school day in December, Alexa walked out the front doors to head home. She was feeling good; she had done most of her homework at lunch, and her English teacher had given her a few new books that she was excited to read. As she stepped outside, the dark chocolate brown skin of her cheeks felt fresh in the cold winter air, and she realized that her perfect ponytail puff had made it through the day. What could be better?

But as soon as she reached the steps outside the door, Alexa tripped, lost her balance, and dropped her new books down the stairs. She bent to pick them up and noticed a shadow stretching over her hands. When she looked up, Natasha and her rat-pack were standing over her.

"What's the matter with you, girl?" Natasha hissed. "You ain't got enough books in that heavy-ass backpack of yours? You need to actually take more books out of the library?" Natasha's two followers laughed.

"Ain't is *not* a word," Alexa thought to herself. But when Natasha and her friends froze and stared at her, Alexa realized that she hadn't just thought that to herself. She had actually said it *out loud*.

"What did you say?" Natasha bellowed. "What did you just say to me, girl?"

Alexa stared back, unable to respond. She was

dreading what Natasha would say next—or worse yet, what she would *do* next. Natasha had been suspended the year before for punching another girl in the face.

But it turns out a punch would have felt better than what actually happened.

"You know what, girls?" Natasha said, loud and slow. They were starting to attract a crowd around the school steps, and Alexa couldn't escape. Natasha waved her pointer finger in the air, threw her head around in a slow deliberate circle, and when she spoke, she practically screamed to the crowd.

"I finally figured out what's wrong with Alexa." she bellowed. "She WHITE!"

"What?" Alexa asked. She didn't know whether to be scared, or angry, or sad. For the moment, she was just shocked.

"You heard me, white girl!" Natasha laughed, now relishing in the attention she was getting from the couple dozen kids watching. "You may think you're white and try to act white all the time, you might even have a white mom now who picks you up from school sometimes, but I've got news for you: YOU'RE BLACK. Get over it."

Half of the kids watching laughed or snickered. The others just stood there.

And then there was Alexa.

She was overwhelmed with sadness and anger. She didn't know what to say. She didn't know what to do. She picked up her books and ran. She ran down the stairs, down the street, and around the corner. Instead of heading to the bus stop, she ran block after block—forty-three blocks, over two miles—until she got to her house. She ran in the cold, stopping only for some NO WALKING signs (not even all of them) and the occasional bike.

When she reached her apartment building, she finally stopped running.

She went upstairs and started thinking. And crying. She stopped to look in the mirror. She liked what she saw most of the time, because she could see all the ways she looked like her mom. But right now, she looked scared and weak. "God, and Mom, please give me the strength to take on the world, and to be me," she prayed as she looked into the bathroom mirror.

Alexa was not going to let Natasha—or anyone—define her. But that didn't make it hurt any less.

She simply couldn't stay at that school. Not an option. She wiped the tears off her face, took out her books, and started doing her homework instead of crying for one more second.

21

David was good at doing homework, but this homework felt even easier than usual. He had already zipped through math, social studies, and English. He studied for his science quiz for a bit, and then finally, his attention turned to his other homework from last week: "Write about a normal family," his therapist had said.

David sat down at the desk in his room, the day before his next therapy session, ready to write. He put on his Mets cap for good luck and stared up at the Mets poster on his wall. The Mets were always a good escape when the going got tough.

"A normal family is two parents who are healthy and loving to their kids," he wrote.

Then he stopped. Just as quickly as he was ready to start writing, he couldn't think of what to write next.

He thought about his friend, Gabriel, whose parents had split when Gabriel was three. He lived with his mom now, and he barely saw his dad. But Gabriel's family seemed pretty normal to him. So he crossed out what he had written and rewrote: "A normal family is one or two parents who are healthy and loving to their kids."

David sat there at his desk, struggling with what else to write. He couldn't think of what else a normal family was, so he tried to think of what it wasn't.

Then he got a text from his mom that reminded him: *Dad's psychotic again. I can't take this anymore. Please watch Dani and Philip. I have to take him to the hospital. Sorry.*

Now *that* was not normal.

But David didn't have time to think of what a normal family was anymore. He had to go take care of his brother and sister.

22

"WAKE UP, BABY! IT'S TIME TO PARTY!"

Tiffany half-smiled to hear her alarm clock go off at 7 a.m. It was hard to be too tired or grumpy when her Wake-Up Call app delivered such funny messages every day.

Tiffany turned to grab the glass of water that she had left for herself the night before, and next to the cup she saw a notecard. She grabbed the card and quickly read it:

"Hey Tiff,

Sorry I gave you a hard time about wanting to go to Hunter. I've been so busy I didn't even give it a chance. The school seems amazing, just like you. Go on, take the test, and keep on making us proud!

Love, Mom

P.S. It's going to be quite a commute!"

Tiffany was beside herself. She hadn't been sure if her mom would come through for her—but in the end she always did! *Except for when it came to dad*, Tiffany thought, *but that's not worth thinking about right now, is it?*

She skipped across the hall and knocked on her parents' bedroom door.

"What is it?" her mom asked sleepily.

"Can I come in?"

"Yep, come on in," Mom replied.

"Thank you, thank you, thank you!" shouted Tiffany as she plopped onto her parents' bed and put her arms around her yawning mom and her still-sleeping dad. "I won't let you down! I really, really, really appreciate both of you, I love both of you, thank—"

"Okay, Tiger," Mom cut her off. "Just keep working hard, like you always do."

Tiffany looked at her mom and felt genuinely grateful. She realized then that she had always idolized her dad and blamed her mom—she wondered if she might have things backward. She glanced over at her dad, still snoring despite all the commotion, and looked closer at the nightstand on his side of the bed: four empty beer cans, a shot glass, and a mostly empty bottle of Tequila.

Tiffany leaned into her mom and sighed. "He didn't even talk to you about the Hunter test, did he?"

Her mom half-smiled and pulled Tiffany close to her chest. She pet her hair gently and slowly, twirling the end of her bright red braid. After a few seconds, she lifted Tiffany's chin to look her in the eyes. She said,

"You just pass that test and go on to do the great things I know you'll do." She gave her a wink and a smile that Tiffany would never forget.

23

Albert was a man on a mission.

Or at least a boy with some serious business to attend to: study like crazy and get into Hunter. He studied after school every single weekday and all day Saturday. The only day Albert took off from studying was Sunday. That was the day his dad usually picked him up, so it was the one day Albert got to relax a little.

Except, of course, that a day with Dad meant a day of his mom and dad fighting at pick-up and drop-off, and there were typically lots of awkward moments. Albert experienced one such moment in the middle of December, soon after he had told Paul the family secret.

He was waiting in his room, reading a book just for fun—the fifth book in the Harry Potter series, to be precise. Dad rang the bell, and before Albert could pop out of his room and race to the door, his mother had answered. Albert stood just inside his bedroom doorway, listening in but hidden from sight.

"Hello, Bob," said Mom. "What are you guys off to do

today?"

"We're going to take it easy today, Shuchun," said Dad. "I'm concerned that Albert is too stressed out about studying for the Hunter test, and I want him to be able to relax."

Albert was curious enough to pop half-out of his room at this point. He wanted to see the action but didn't want to have to deal with it.

"Are you being critical of my parenting, Bob?" asked Mom, crossing her arms. "Because I thought we agreed that Albert getting into Hunter is the best chance he has to get into a good college and become the successful man we know he can become!"

"No, Shuchun, I agree with you," replied Dad. "It's just that, well, I've learned this year that there are things more important than school and work. I want our son to be successful, but more importantly, I want him to be well-adjusted. I want him to be happy, Shuchun. Don't you?"

Albert saw his mom raise her eyebrows and lift her clenched fist up toward her head. He was afraid of what that kind of anger might mean. He thought he should probably interrupt this conversation, but he wanted to see where it would lead.

"Of course I want him to be happy, Bob," replied Mom. "Getting into Hunter will help him get into a great college, which will help him get a great job like a doctor or engineer, which will make him money. And then, he will be successful and happy."

"It's just not that simple, Shuchun," Dad said through clenched teeth. "And another thing: Guillermo and I think we should talk about having Albert see a therapist. To talk about his feelings about our divorce and my coming out, and how it's all affected him. You know?" Dad held his hands out to Mom, but she didn't take them. Her face was getting redder and redder by the second.

Albert cringed. He knew it was bad enough for his dad to suggest to his mom that there were more important things than studying. But to suggest that he should see a *therapist*? For one thing, people he knew just didn't see therapists. And to make it even worse, Dad had mentioned Guillermo. No, this was not going to be good at all.

"WHAT?!" shrieked Mom. "You want our son to go to some shrink?! Whose idea was that? Your boyfriend's? And who's going to pay for the shrink? What's going to happen when he wastes all his time talking about his feelings and doesn't study? He won't get into Hunter, he won't get into a good college, and he won't get a job. And then, Bob, *then* he will need a therapist! But for now, no, that is not what our son needs. You want to help? Pay for another tutor! This conversation is over." She turned back toward the hall. "Albert! Your father's here!"

That was his cue. Albert grabbed his coat from his room and sprinted to his father, pretending that he hadn't heard that whole conversation—though at the volume his parents had been speaking, it was probably pretty obvious that he had.

"Hey, Dad! What's up?" Albert asked, trying his best to break the tension.

"Good to see you, son," Dad said and smiled at Albert. Then he turned to Albert's mom. "This conversation may be over for you, Shuchun, but it's not over for me. We'll talk more about this later." He turned back to Albert. "Come on, Albert, let's go. Today is a day to rest and relax."

It didn't seem very relaxing so far!

24

It had been two days since Natasha had called Alexa "white" in front of the whole school, and Alexa still hadn't told her dad. She wanted to, but she also didn't want to bother him with a problem that he couldn't fix.

Still, it kept nagging at her. Sure, she had been teased in school before, especially this year when she had been studying harder, and the kids seemed like they were just getting meaner. But nobody had ever called her "white." It just felt like the cruelest insult; like her mom was gone and now her Blackness was disappearing too.

Alexa paced around the living room table, bobbing her head up and down, amping herself up to that old Drake song "Started from the Bottom"—one of her mom and dad's favorites. The beat always got her going. She had made up her mind. She was going to talk to her dad about what happened at school. It was a Thursday, and her dad was usually home by six. Celia was meeting her sister to do a weekly catch-up over manicures, which meant she wouldn't be home until around eight. Plenty of time.

But then a funny thing happened: it was her step-mother, Celia, who came home first.

"Hello there, Alexa!" called Celia as she bounded through the door, dropping her briefcase and sitting on the corner of the couch. "I came home early today to try to steal some time with you, my dear!" The Grinch batted her eyelashes as if she were a fairy who had come to enchant Alexa and shower her with pixie dust. All Alexa could see was Celia ruining her chance to have a night alone with her dad.

"Um, o-okay, Celia," Alexa stammered. Celia was gazing across the room at Alexa, but Alexa couldn't look Celia in the eye. She was too overwhelmed with feelings that she couldn't explain in that moment.

Where is my dad? was running through Alexa's mind. She looked down at her feet and tried to contain herself. "I have a lot of homework, so I'm not sure I can spend much time with you right now, Celia. Sorry." She looked back up at Celia, trying her best to look sad.

"That's okay!" Celia smiled at Alexa with a twinkle in her eyes.

Celia, the living doll, Alexa thought. Celia's hair was always perfectly curled, her outfits always perfectly matching. Alexa wished Celia would perfectly pack up her bags and leave her and her dad alone. But she knew that wasn't going to happen. Celia was her stepmother for better or for worse. Alexa had been the ring bearer at her dad's wedding. *Ugh. . . .* Alexa opened her math book.

There was an awkward silence in the living room. The TV was off, and Alexa was working on a math equation; she could see Celia barely making her way through an old magazine as she kept throwing bright-eyed, inquisitive looks Alexa's way.

A little later, when Alexa was about halfway through her math homework, Celia got up and glided into the kitchen. As the door swung back and forth, the Grinch sang out, "So, you know, if you want to talk about anything or you need help with your homework, I'm here, okay?" Alexa could hear her opening the refrigerator. "And don't worry. I'll stay quiet if you don't want to talk. You won't even know I'm here." She walked out of the kitchen a couple of minutes later and handed Alexa her favorite drink: lemonade, in her favorite Spider-Man cup.

Lemonade? thought Alexa. *My Spider-Man cup? The Grinch is always trying to get on my good side. Good luck, lady! She shouldn't just assume I want lemonade. . . . I mean, I do want lemonade, but . . . ugh.*

Alexa took the glass of lemonade and looked up at Celia. "Um, okay . . . thanks," she said as she put down her glass. She watched Celia sit back down nearby, smiling at her. Alexa looked back down at her notebook. She didn't want to be talking to Celia right now, or ever. She wanted to do her homework, and if she was going to talk to anyone, she wanted it to be her dad.

After a few seconds, Celia leaned in and asked, "So, how was your day?"

"Celia!" Alexa snapped, no longer trying to hide how annoyed she was. "You literally just said you'd leave me alone, and like two seconds later you're asking me about my day! What's the deal?"

"I know, I know, I'm sorry," said Celia. "It's just that, well, I care about you, Alexa. And I noticed for the last couple of days you haven't been acting like yourself. So . . ." Celia sat up straight and smiled, "I don't know if something is the matter and that maybe you don't want to talk to your dad about? Girl stuff?" She shrugged. "I know it's probably hard to talk to your dad about some things, but I'm here. And our whole situation—me and your dad—it's hard. It's new. But I want you to know that I care about you and I'm here if you want or need to talk. Okay?"

Alexa didn't respond. She looked at her lemonade and then over at Celia, who had buried her face in the pages of that old magazine again.

Alexa remembered the first time she had seen her dad smile after her mom had passed away. He hadn't cracked a smile or a silly joke in over two years. Their apartment had all but fallen silent, and their days were a cycle of the same activities: takeout, homework, church, and TV. Then one day, Dad had come home with big smile on his face, pulled out his old skillet, and made Alexa his "famous" grilled cheese for the first time in over two years. That was the day that Daddy had met Celia. That was the day that everything had changed. Alexa wasn't sure why she hated Celia so much. She just knew she was hurting . . .

she missed her mom, and now she missed her dad as well.

For the next half hour or so, Alexa just pretended to do her homework, but her mind was racing with what Natasha had said to her and what it meant.

Her dad was always teaching Alexa about what he called "the real American history," the plights that Black American people face and have faced. But Dad never talked badly about anyone white in particular, and he had married Celia.

Alexa didn't know a lot of white people personally, other than Celia. There were a couple of white kids at her school, but they never hung out. There was her PE teacher, Mr. Vertel. Oh, and, of course, Lorraine, Mom's best friend from the building. But that was about it. She had never had a bad experience with a white person, but she knew from Natasha's tone that calling her white was an insult.

When Alexa's dad came home about a half an hour later, Alexa was still pretending to do her homework, and Celia was still pretending to flip through magazines.

"Hello, my two most favorite ladies!" Dad said, smiling as he came through the door, tossed his bag, and locked the apartment door behind him.

"Hi, honey. How's your brother? Celia asked.

"He's good. He says hello." Dad answered.

Before anyone could say another word, Alexa leapt up and jumped into her father's arms. "Dad, finally! You're home!" She grabbed him tightly around his waist. She was still so upset about Natasha she started to shake when her father hugged her back.

"Hey, baby girl. You're shaking! What's the matter?"

Celia closed the magazine on her lap and looked over at Alexa. "Are you okay?" she asked.

Alexa sighed. She looked up to her dad, over to Celia, and back again. Alexa didn't want Celia around for this discussion, but she was all torn up and couldn't hold back for another second.

She decided to take a chance.

"Dad," Alexa said. "Celia . . ."

"What's the matter, Lex?" Dad asked as he hugged Alexa a bit tighter. "You look like you've seen a ghost."

"It's worse than that, Dad. Natasha, at school . . . she called me white," Alexa blurted out.

"*What*?" Her dad pulled himself back and looked Alexa straight in the eyes, dumbfounded. "What did you just say?"

"Nothing." Alexa was breathing heavily. "I mean, she's called me names before and stuff, but this time . . . well, she called me white in a mean way, and it really hurt my feelings."

Alexa looked over at Celia, who was as pale as could be, and felt bad for a moment. "I mean, there's nothing wrong with being white, of course," she said in Celia's direction. "But I'm not white, I'm Black. You know, I have a Black dad. And . . . and . . . I had a Black mom." Alexa began to cry.

Alexa's dad led her to the couch and sat next to her. He rubbed Alexa's shoulder. "Oh, Alexa. I am so sorry," he said. "That must have been terrible." He wiped a tear from Alexa's eye. "Natasha's a mean girl. And you have every right to be upset, angry, hurt . . . all of the things."

"I knew something was wrong," Celia chimed in. "I am so sorry, sweetheart."

Alexa sniffled. "Thanks, Celia. But it's . . . complicated. I'm Black and I'm proud of it." She couldn't stop the tears from falling from her eyes. "But I don't want to be around people who are going to bully me and be mean just because I take school seriously. I want to be around people who lift me up. Who are nice."

"I understand, sweetie." Dad answered.

"I want to go to the best school. I want to go to Hunter. But I don't want to go there if it's going to make people think I don't want to be Black."

Alexa's dad put his arm around her, and she laid her head on his shoulder. "Going to a new school like Hunter and leaving the neighborhood won't make you white, baby girl. I promise," he said. "You are a beautiful Black girl who is going to grow up into a beautiful Black woman, you understand? This is your home, where you're from, your roots. Nothing can change that. Not even Nasty Natasha . . . can we call her that?" He chuckled. "Better yet, let's not call her at all. Hunter is going to be challenging, and very new, and very different. Celia and I just want you to be ready if you get in."

"*When* I get in," Alexa corrected him. She was emotionally spent, but she smiled for a small moment before the tears fell again.

They all sat in silence for a few minutes while Alexa cried it out.

Once Alexa had caught her breath again, she looked up and asked, "Is it okay if I go to my room for a little while, Dad?"

"Sure, sweetie. Of course. We'll give you some space. And we can all discuss what we're going to do about this Natasha situation over dinner. It's going to be okay. I promise." Dad answered.

Alexa picked up her books and began to walk toward her bedroom.

"Hey, Alexa," Celia called out. "That Hunter test is going to be a piece of cake!"

Alexa turned back toward Celia and nodded.

When she got into her room, she had to crack a little smile, because she knew that—for the first time since she'd met her—Celia was right.

25

It had been about a month since David had started going to therapy sessions with Mary, and things were going a lot better than he'd expected.

David liked having a place to go where somebody would listen to him. For fifty minutes, it wasn't about his sick dad or his overwhelmed mom or taking care of his little brother and sister. It was just about him.

More importantly, he felt like he was learning some valuable skills: how to express his feelings a bit better without breaking down into tears, and how to slow down a bit and breathe when feeling flooded.

But it wasn't making life at home or at school much easier. Life at home was chaotic, to say the least, and life at school was still challenging; his dad was still sick, Tony was still a jerk, and David was focused on studying for this Hunter test.

He had done some research online, and it looked like Hunter was a really good school. It was far away from his house in Brooklyn—all the way on the Upper East Side of Manhattan. To get there, David would have to walk to the subway and then take two different trains. It would take over an hour to get to school. But based on the online reviews, it seemed awesome. David figured he should study hard to at least get in, and he could decide later what to do.

The biggest challenge was that David was doing this alone. He knew his parents loved him and all, but they were busy dealing with Dad's bipolar disorder. It was a strange illness—it meant that sometimes Dad got really depressed and sad, and other times he was super happy, but not in touch with reality. Actually, that part was the scariest, like when he had run out into the street months earlier, screaming for Mom. It was all too overwhelming to think about; much more overwhelming than getting ready for the Hunter test. So David focused on the test, researched what would be on it and how to study for it, and set himself a studying schedule.

Since David had Hebrew school on Tuesdays and Thursdays, he studied every Monday and Wednesday after school and all afternoon on Saturdays. He was impressed with himself for being as disciplined as he was. There were always distractions: the obvious ones, like his siblings and parents, but also . . . video games.

David was the best Fortnite player in his whole school. And sure, that seemed to only make Tony tease him more about being a nerd, but it was something David was really proud of. Tony might have been an a-hole, but David knew that most of the other kids respected him for his Fortnite prowess.

On this particular Saturday afternoon, after a solid hour of studying, David got the urge to play. It was incredible to live in a different world (if only for fifteen minutes) where he could have friends and support and weapons to help him win battles. It felt good to have friends, even if it wasn't the kind you saw at school. When David played, his dad's illness and the bullies at school didn't matter at all. All that mattered was the battle.

David opened up the app on his phone and set up a game. As he waited for the hundred other players to join to start the battle, he realized how similar this was to taking the Hunter test: many people would try, but only one in a hundred of them could emerge victorious in the Battle Royale. That was about the odds of getting into Hunter; three thousand kids took the test, and only 150 got in.

The battle began. David found a good shelter, got some weapons, made a few kills, and quickly made it to the final twenty people. Within a few more minutes, he was cruising his way to victory. Fourteen people left . . . twelve . . . seven . . . and then a sniper snuck up on David and took him out. Just like that, he went from cruising his way to victory to dead as a dormouse.

Oh well, he thought to himself. *There's always next game.*

Of course, when it came to the Hunter test, there would be no "next game" if David failed.

He put down his phone, stretched his arms up above his head, and then picked up his study guide, determined to face a real-life battle.

And that's exactly what David did.

26

Tiffany was not going to let this opportunity go to waste.

Every day since she had gotten that note from her mom, she would come straight home after school and get right to studying. She didn't want to follow the path that she had seen her big sister go down. At first it seemed like no big deal—her sister just wanted to hang out with her friends instead of doing her homework. I mean, who liked homework anyway? No one! But pretty soon, Tiffany's sister was out with her friends every night, and going to parties and drinking every Friday and Saturday night. Sometimes she was getting drunk, just like Dad, and she was only in the tenth grade!

No, Tiffany did *not* want to follow in her sister's foot-steps. And guess where her sister went to high school? Bayside, the same school that her mom went to and the same school that she was set to go to—unless Tiffany could change that plan.

The only thing she could do was study as hard as she

could. The rest of her life seemed to be out of her control, and it seemed like lately things were even more out-of-control than ever. Dad was out drinking six nights a week, her sister was out partying four or five nights a week, and Mom was, well, checked out. Tiffany knew she was trying. *But boy*, she thought. *You get ignored enough, and it's hard to feel like anybody cares.*

Where did that leave Tiffany? It left her pretty much on her own, studying, going to school, and making breakfast and dinner. It seemed like her sister was growing up too fast, and sometimes Tiffany felt like she was growing up too fast herself, but in a different way. Was it in a good way?

At the moment, it didn't matter. It was 7 p.m. and it was study time. The Hunter test was next week, and Tiffany wasn't sure if she was good enough, smart enough, or lucky enough to get in. All she knew was that it was worth a shot. So she sat in her kitchen by herself, on a Thursday night, studying test-prep books she had bought with her own money.

Studying was hard that night. Mom was on an overnight shift at the hospital, and she could only guess where her sister and her father were. It was weird—sometimes when she was alone in the house, and everything was quiet, that was actually the hardest time to study.

Tiffany took out her phone for some company and opened up Instagram. A quick scroll through her feed and it seemed like everyone was having more fun than she was, as usual. Everyone was smiling, hanging out with friends, going on awesome adventures, and going to the coolest places in New York.

Why was everyone else having so much more fun than Tiffany? Why was everyone so perfect on social media? Sometimes Tiffany wondered if any of them had their own secrets, or problems, or drunk dads and party-animal sisters. But story after story told her otherwise.

She closed Instagram and looked at the time. It was 8:45! Where had all of the time gone? Tiffany could not believe how much time she had just wasted looking through her feed. And for what?

I'm stronger than this! Tiffany thought to herself. *I should be studying.* She looked around her, at the home she'd known her whole life, and she started to dream. *I could be a lawyer like the women on* Law and Order, she thought, *or start my own show* . . . The Tiffany Cacciatore Chef Show! Tiffany laughed to herself, then looked down at her phone. *What am I doing on Instagram?* she thought. *This is the perfect time for me to study. Why am I wasting it?*

And then Tiffany did something she literally had never done since getting her phone a year ago: she shut her phone off. She picked up her test-prep books, went downstairs, and settled into her dad's recliner. She knew she could study peacefully for a couple of hours. Plus, Tiffany liked to make sure her dad got home safely before she went to bed, so she was in the right place for that. He couldn't possibly miss her if she was in his chair when he came home.

Tiffany turned on the lamp beside her and got to it: Chapter One, Language Arts. . . .

She didn't realize that she had fallen asleep. When she woke up, she was still in her dad's recliner, but now there was a soft blanket on top of her and a pillow under her head; the TV and lamp were off, and the lights up the stairs were on.

Tiffany's mind was half asleep. She looked around. She saw her test-prep books on the coffee table with her highlighters and pens. And there was a glass of water. Tiffany smiled. She got up, folded the blanket, went up to her room, got into her bed, and turned her phone back on to check the time. It was 1:30 a.m.

When she closed her eyes, her dreams were filled with her own Instagram story: one where she was sitting back, acing the Hunter test.

27

Albert had been studying so much his brain hurt. He was grateful when Dad and Guillermo told him to take a break for the night. They were going to get dim sum and then watch a movie (a PG-13 movie that Albert's mom would never have let him watch).

Albert sat down at the table at Jing Fong, his favorite traditional-style Chinese restaurant in Chinatown, and got ready for round one of dim sum.

"So, how's school?" asked Dad.

"It's good, I guess," replied Albert. "I've been studying a lot for the Hunter test next week."

"Sounds like you really want to go to Hunter," said Dad.

"Of course!" said Albert. "Just about everyone in my class is taking the test. I just want to make you and Mom proud, you know? Go to Hunter, go to an Ivy League school, become a doctor or lawyer or engineer. I'm on it."

"You know," said Guillermo, "you don't have to go to Hunter. You don't have to become a doctor or engineer.

You don't have to go to an Ivy League school." He paused to glance at Albert's dad, who nodded. Then he turned back to Albert and leaned close. "You don't even have to go to college! I'm just saying, my dad is a plastic surgeon, and that's what I had planned to be my entire life. That was the plan. I got into undergrad for pre-med and everything. But the first day I had to dissect something, *that* was over." Guillermo screwed his face up, pretending like he was going to be sick as he grabbed at his stomach and rolled his eyes. "So, I dropped out of Columbia University." He laughed. "Boy, oh boy! That made nobody happy. I was out of school and out of work, but I was still fascinated by what my father did and started dabbling in makeup. Look where that's gotten me! Who knew I'd end up becoming the owner of my own makeup line? It took some time, but now I'm opening my third shop in New York City and one in Los Angeles. See Albert? And I'm a college dropout!" Guillermo turned to Dad and chuckled with a wide-eyed, goofy grin. Dad smiled back at Guillermo, then watched Albert.

Albert took a bite of his dumpling and thought for a moment. "Well, Guillermo," Albert replied, "Don't take this the wrong way, but I don't think I want be a college dropout or own my own makeup line. I mean, I think I want to be a doctor. And I mean, I definitely want to go to Hunter!"

Albert immediately felt bad. But, honestly, who was Guillermo to tell him that his plan wasn't going to work?

Albert knew what his mom and dad wanted of him and he knew he wanted to make his parents proud. Guillermo was a nice guy and everything, but he didn't understand. He was Puerto Rican, for one thing—the only Puerto Rican person Albert knew except people he'd seen on TV. And he was gay. He didn't understand Albert's life.

"Look, Albert," his dad said, reaching across the table and tussling Albert's hair, "whatever school you go to, and whatever you become when you grow up, I'll be proud of you. Even if you drop out of school and want to play with makeup like Guillermo," he chuckled.

It was time for more dumplings (and more thinking) for Albert. He reached across the table and took three freshly-made pork dumplings that the waiter had just brought over, and put them on his plate. He looked up to the ceiling as he chewed, as if he was having a conversation with a friend in the sky. This was weird—his mom and dad had always said they wanted Albert to study hard, go to a good high school like Hunter, go to an Ivy League school for college, and become a doctor or engineer. That was just the way it had always been.

Until a year and ten months ago, that was. It seemed like since Dad had met Guillermo and discovered he was gay, he had also become more like the people outside of their community circle that his classmates made fun of. Like the kids in their class who didn't go to tutoring and weren't taking the Hunter test next week. Albert had always thought that those parents didn't care about their kids' education. And now, it seemed like Guillermo and Dad didn't care either.

The dumpling house was chaotic as always. Loud waiters were coming from every direction, steam was rising up from bamboo baskets on the tables, and a line was forming at the front door. But Albert was lost in his thoughts. "You must really love that dumpling," Guillermo interrupted Albert's thinking. He smiled another one of his silly smiles. "Or else you're really that terrified of ending up a *loser* makeup artist like me." Guillermo was always joking, but this time, even Albert's dad put down his dumpling, turned to Guillermo, and raised his brows.

"No, no, I'm not scared of becoming a makeup artist," stammered Albert, who felt even worse than before. "I mean, that just came out wrong. I'm not saying you're a loser, Guillermo. It's just weird, you know? This is different from what Mom and Dad have always said. It's not normal, you know?"

Guillermo put down his dumpling. "Sure, Albert. But what is 'normal'?" he asked. "I know it's strange, the idea of things being different from what you've been told. Or how you think they should be. You're still not used to *this* either," he continued as he pointed to Dad and back to himself with his chopsticks. "But take it from me. I've learned the hard way, over forty years of being a gay man in a straight person's world: normal is just a setting on a washing machine, Albert. Just be kind and follow your heart."

Chinatown was its own city on the island of Manhattan, both smaller and more crowded than you can imagine. People like Guillermo stuck out. He was a high-fashion guy; he had a slicked-back, symmetrical haircut, and he wore crisp, brightly colored linen shirts unbuttoned halfway down his chest and a long gold necklace with a cross on it. He was loud a lot of the time and proud to be. He was different. He was most certainly not normal to Albert. *But maybe he's right*, thought Albert. Maybe he didn't have to go to Hunter or Harvard or become a doctor. *Maybe . . .*

"What Guillermo is trying to say," said Dad, "is that things change. I know I always told you I wanted you to study hard and go to a good school and make me proud. And all of that is still true. But, well, I realized when I met Guillermo that you can be happy doing anything you want. And now, I can honestly tell you I will be equally proud of you whether you get into Hunter or not."

"Well, why am I studying four hours a day for this, Dad?!" Albert put down his chopsticks, clenched his fists, and looked down at the table. He didn't want to make any eye contact at the moment.

"Because that's what you've always known, Albert," said Dad. "And that's totally okay too! But what I'm saying is that either way, it will be okay."

Albert was confused. This wasn't the dad he had known for eleven years. It was a completely new dad. He tried to brush it off, to think about the movie they were going to watch and the three hours of fun time remaining before he had to get back to his mom and his studying.

"Thanks, Dad and Guillermo," he said out loud. "A lot to think about. But for now, more dim sum!"

28

Alexa sat at her desk and pulled her Jimi Hendrix shirt over her knees. She was baffled. It seemed like just yesterday she had found out she was going to take the Hunter test, and now it was just days away. The time had gone by too quickly.

Alexa asked everyone she knew if they had heard about this "special school in a castle in the city." Everyone in Sunday school responded by laughing and asking Alexa if she had read about this school in one of those comic books she was always reading. No one from her middle school knew about it. Her auntie had heard of Hunter, but that was it. None of her cousins in Flatbush had heard of Hunter either.

Still, as she sat at home doing her homework, she felt more excited and confident than scared. She was determined to make her mom proud in heaven.

"Knock, knock," Alexa heard through the crack in her bedroom door, along with an actual knock and a smiling face. It was her dad.

Alexa smiled. "Hey, Dad. What's up?"

He opened the door wider and took a step in. "Nothing. I'm just checking in. How's your homework going?"

She rolled her eyes. "Bor-ing," she sighed.

"Of course it's boring! It's homework!" Dad laughed as he shot finger guns at Alexa with a "Pew-pew!" Then he walked in and put his arm around Alexa's shoulder. "How are you feeling about the Hunter test?" he asked.

"I'm okay." Alexa shrugged. "I just don't really know anyone who's taken it, so I don't know quite what to expect."

"Well, what do I always tell you to do when you don't know something?"

Alexa smiled and rolled her eyes again. "Google it," she said.

So she googled on her phone: "What to expect when taking the Hunter test," and scrolled through the results.

But her answer didn't pop up. Instead, there were all sorts of pop-up ads for tutors and test prep programs to get in!

Alexa winced. It was intimidating. It was over-whelming. It was terrifying!

Alexa's mood had changed from confident to pan-icked in an instant. "Dad, I'm kinda freaking out here," said Alexa. "Seems like everyone is hiring a tutor or taking some sort of special program to get into this school. The test is in four days! I don't have time for that. What am I gonna do?" She pulled her legs out from under her shirt and started to rub her belly as she continued to scroll . . . anything to make her head stop spinning.

Her dad lifted Alexa's face away from her phone screen and up to his. "Honey, I know it feels scary," he said, "but I can promise you that most of the kids who take the test did not hire an expensive tutor. They just didn't. And obviously, I was wrong this one time; don't google it!"

Alexa laughed, but inside she was really shaken. Why hadn't Dad thought to get her a tutor? Why hadn't *she* thought to *ask* for a tutor? Alexa was normally smarter than this.

"And another thing," Dad continued. "These types of tests don't test how much you can memorize. They test how smart you are. That's why you'll shine!"

"Thanks, Dad, but I don't feel very shiny right now."

Dad looked her in the eyes and said firmly, "You. Will. Shine. I just know it."

"Okay," Alexa repeatedly cynically, "I will shine."

Her dad stood up and faced her. "No, really! You will! Now repeat after me: I will shine."

Alexa thought this whole exercise was stupid, but she played along for her dad's sake. "I will shine," she said again, and couldn't help but smile a little.

"Say it like you mean it!" Dad shouted.

Alexa's smile grew. "I will shine!" she shouted and fell onto her bed. She sighed. "Dad, you're so corny!"

They laughed together. Her dad picked her up and

spun her around in the air before landing her back on top of her pillows. She couldn't stop smiling.

As her dad was walking out of her room, Alexa said, "Hey, Dad? Grandpa Jacob says I have Mommy's nose. Do you think so?"

Her dad laughed. "You sure do," he said. "Luckily, you don't snore like her though."

"Ha! Now, can you *please* get out of my room?"

He winked. "Sure, I can do that."

And he did.

29

It was a big day: the first Monday in January, and the first day David would ever travel to Manhattan by himself. He was super nervous, but excited too. He put on his Mets jacket and opened up the front door of his Brooklyn home to begin his journey. The jacket wasn't quite warm enough on this cold, cloudy day, but he had to wear it for good luck. He had plotted out the whole trip on his HopStop subway app and left an hour early, just to be safe.

David was sad to be doing this alone, but his father was sick, and his mom needed to work. He kept his head down, walked three blocks to get to the 53rd Street R train subway stop, took the A train to Atlantic Avenue, and then transferred to the 4 train, which he took to 86th Street in Manhattan, and then transferred to the local 6 train for one stop to 96th Street. Then he walked another three blocks to get to the large, castle-like, brick building that was Hunter High School.

After the hour-and-twenty-minute subway ride, David was breathing faster than normal, but he was unsure if that was from exhaustion, nervousness, or excitement. After weeks of studying, David felt ready. Most of all, after months of being teased for being a nerd at school, David felt ready to change his life.

He looked at the crowd of people outside the school and couldn't believe it! First of all, David was an hour early, and still there was a crowd of people already there. That seemed crazy. Also, he couldn't help but notice that it looked like at least eighty percent of all the kids there were Asian.

Then, there were all of the adults. David had suspected that most sixth graders would be there with one of their parents, and he had tried to prepare himself to deal with that. But faced with the reality, it was harder than he thought it would be. It seemed like most kids there had their mom or dad with them, and some of them had both! David drooped his shoulders as he entered the building.

He made his way to the front desk in the main lobby. "Last name?" asked the older, gray-haired woman with glasses at the desk, barely looking up from the printed list in her hands.

"Kaplan," said David.

She scanned the list with her pointer finger and stopped at his name. "Okay, David, you're in room 202." She looked up at him and pointed to the stairs behind him. "One flight up and to the right. The test begins in fifty-four minutes, but you can head to the room now if you want." She cracked a smile. "Good luck!"

David thanked her and headed up the stairs. He still couldn't believe how crowded it was. When he arrived in room 202, there were already twelve kids there. It was an unremarkable classroom, except for a poster in the front of the room, which read, "You are not normal."

David sat down in the back row, in between a tall Asian kid and, now that he thought about it, the only African American girl he had seen since he had gotten off the subway at 96th Street. She was cute, with a sweet smile and curly black hair in one perfect puff on top of her head.

He felt really overwhelmed, but then he thought about what he'd learned in therapy. He took a deep breath to pause and recognize the feeling before letting it pass. Then, he could start a conversation.

"Hi, I'm David," he said to the girl. "What's your name?"

"Hi, David. I'm Alexa," she replied. "Nice to meet you."

David turned to his right and was about to introduce himself when the tall kid did it first. "Hey, David," he said, "I'm Albert."

"Nice to meet you both. Albert, this is Alexa," said David as he looked at each of them. "You guys nervous?"

"Uh, yeah!" replied Alexa. "There's like a million kids here, and I heard it's almost impossible to get in."

"Three thousand," said Albert with a straight face. "That's not quite a million. But yeah, I'm nervous too."

"I've been studying," said David. "But it feels like a lot of people have been."

Albert sighed. "Yeah, I mean, I've been going to the tutoring center four days a week for, like, two years to get ready for this. It's out of control!" he said with his eyes wide.

They all laughed nervously. David gulped. Two years? That was a lifetime. He turned to Alexa, who smiled awkwardly at him as if to say, "I didn't have a tutor either."

The room filled up as the time ticked closer and closer to the test.

"We'll begin in ten minutes," said the test proctor at the front of the room, an older man with glasses and very little hair. "As you know, there will be no latecomers entering the room, and no bathroom breaks. So, if you need to use the bathroom, please use it now."

Strangely, nobody got up. Maybe everybody was too nervous. Ten minutes moved slowly to five and then three. Just as they were about to start, one more girl entered the room, out of breath. She had clearly been running. She sat down in the one empty seat in the room, right in front of David.

"Hey there, way to make it on time!" David whispered to the back of her head.

The girl turned around. "Barely!" she whispered back. "Hi, I'm Tiffany."

"I'm David. Good luck on the test."

"Okay, no more talking, kids," said the proctor. "The test begins now."

30

Tiffany woke up early on the day of the big Hunter test. She had mapped out the path to the school from her home in northeastern Queens, and it wasn't going to be easy. First, she had to take a public bus nine stops to the nearest subway station, then a subway ride into Manhattan, and then transfer to a different subway number to get to the school on 94th Street.

She felt alone but determined. Tiffany was the only girl from her school taking the test, and since her parents both had to work, she was on her own getting there.

She brushed her teeth, put on some clothes, and headed to the kitchen to grab cereal. There on the kitchen table was a note from her mom: "Good luck, Tiff. You will do great. XO, Mom."

She smiled. She went to the cabinet and took out the box of Honey Nut Cheerios. Then she went into the refrigerator to get milk. There was half a roasted chicken left uncovered on the top shelf, a clear container of orange juice with barely a drop in it on the bottom shelf, and . . .

No, no, not the milk!

The carton had been left open with her sister's lipstick all over the top, and, of course, it was empty. Tiffany looked around the empty kitchen and thought, *There must be something more than this. Today, the world is mine for the taking.* She quickly made a couple of peanut butter and jelly sandwiches, took a vitamin water from the fridge, and grabbed the twenty on the counter that her parents had left for lunch.

She checked her phone. *7:15 already? Better get moving!* She grabbed her jacket and headed out the door on her journey to the big city. Tiffany walked to the end of her street, waited ten minutes at the bus stop, and hopped on the Q28 bus to travel to the Flushing-Main St. subway station. There, she transferred from the 7 train to the W train, and at Lexington Avenue and 59th Street in Manhattan, she would take the 6 train up to the school.

Everything was going so well . . . until Tiffany realized she had gotten on the wrong 6 train and was heading downtown instead of uptown!

Oh no, this can't be happening! she screamed in her head. She realized that the ticket out of her neighborhood and on to a better life was being ripped up in her face with every minute that went by. She quickly got a hold of herself, got off at the next stop, and raced up the stairs.

Tiffany saw another train coming. She wasn't sure it was going in the right direction, but she didn't have time to check the map. She decided to go with her gut and hop on. She sprinted to the train and got in just as the doors were closing.

"Excuse me," she managed to huff to a stranger on the train, "are we headed uptown?"

"Yep," answered the stranger, never looking up from his phone. Tiffany fell against the subway doors and let out a sigh of relief. She took a look around, found an open seat, took off her backpack, and sat down.

She had the biggest test of her life in minutes, and she was already exhausted. *Why am I alone on this trip?* she thought. *Why couldn't my mom or dad take just one day off to come with me? Hell, they would have only had to take off the morning.*

96th Street came soon, and Tiffany was going to be barely on time for the test—she had to run. When she turned the corner on Park Avenue, she saw the school for the first time. It was massive. It looked like a real-life Rapunzel might live inside. But she didn't have time to think about that. She crossed the street and felt a huge pang of relief as she raced through the doors of the school building only five minutes before the test began.

Thankfully, there was no line at the front desk. Tiffany hurried up to the desk, moving so fast she tripped as she blurted out, "Hi! Tiffany Molly Russo here!"

"Hello there, Tiffany," said the white-haired woman at the desk, unfazed by Tiffany's stumble. The woman scanned through her pages. "Glad to meet you. Now wipe that sweat off your cheek and head on upstairs to room 202."

"Thanks!" shouted Tiffany. She had made it in time! *YES! YES! YES!*

Tiffany was in such a hurry she almost fell over herself twice going up the stairs. She found room 202 easily and hurried inside the door. It was quiet and crowded. She saw one seat open in the back of the room and sat down.

"Hey there, way to make it on time!" she heard the boy right behind her whisper.

She turned around to see him and smiled. "Barely!" she replied. "Hi, I'm Tiffany."

He smiled back at her. "I'm David," he whispered. "Good luck on the test."

Tiffany turned back around to see the test in front of her. With a deep breath in and a deep breath out, she waited to start on the test that could change her life.

31

It was the day Albert had been preparing for all of his life. His dad had taken off from work to take him there, and his mom was going into work late so she could be home when he left that morning.

"Morning, Mom," said Albert, stretching his arms above his head to wake himself up as he appeared in the kitchen.

"Good morning, my son!" she replied. "Have you studied enough?"

"Yes, Mom." Albert chuckled.

"You need to have a very good breakfast," she continued. "I've made you eggs, fresh juice, red bean buns, and tea."

"Thanks, Mom. You're the best."

"Come, let's eat," she answered. "Your father will be here soon to take you to Hunter. This is the one thing he and I are in total agreement about."

Mom cracked a rare smile. Was she proud of him? She wasn't going to say it, but Albert could still feel it. Albert sat down at the table and dug into the scrumptious breakfast his mom had prepared. The doorbell rang.

"Hello, Bob," said Mom when she answered the door. "Come in and have breakfast with us."

Albert watched and smiled as his dad came in and sat down at the kitchen table with them. He couldn't believe how friendly they were being to each other. *Guess today really is special*, he thought.

"We should get going soon, don't you think?" said Dad a few minutes later.

Mom nodded. "Yes. It's time, Albert. You are ready. Now make your parents proud."

Albert looked at his mom and dad, sitting together like they used to when he was little, and said, "You got it."

He stood up, took his plate over to the sink, turned around, and leaned in to give his mom a big hug. She never cried, but he could swear he saw a tear in her right eye as he pulled away from her embrace.

Dad took Albert uptown on the 6 train subway line, and they arrived a half-hour later at Hunter.

Albert knew so many of the families there! It seemed like not only all of Chinatown was there, but also all of Flushing and Brooklyn Chinatown. There were a few non-Asian kids too, but most of all, he was amazed at how many Chinese and Korean kids there were. Albert didn't know there were that many Asian kids in all of New York City! He wasn't sure whether to feel reassured or overwhelmed by this, so he decided to feel reassured, and stood up tall as he got into the line to get into the building.

Albert continued to look around when he was in line. He saw kids from his own class in line and moving through the hallways once he entered the building. Then he got a tap on the shoulder.

"Good luck, kid!" Paul said. "You've got this!"

"Hey, Paul," said Albert. "Good luck to you too!"

Seeing his friend gave Albert a burst of happiness. Now he felt more confident than nervous. He knew he had studied and prepared a lot for this day, and he was ready to make it happen for himself. He finished registering at the front of the line and said goodbye to his dad.

"Good luck, Albert," Dad said. "I'll be waiting for you when you finish the test."

"Thanks, Dad," he replied.

Albert headed upstairs to room 202. He sat in the last seat of the last row of chairs in the back of the room. There was a girl already sitting in the back row, one seat away to his left. They nodded at each other when he sat down. The room was still pretty empty. Albert sat and watched as students trickled in and took their seats. Everybody looked a little nervous.

A little later, a chubby white boy in a Mets jacket sat down in the seat next to Albert. The boy spoke to the girl next to him. Albert turned to introduce himself. He learned that the boy's name was David, and the girl's name was Alexa. The three of them started chatting about how many kids were taking the same test.

"Yeah," said Albert, "I mean, I've been going to the tutoring center four days a week for like two years to get ready for this. It's out of control!"

He saw the boy and the girl exchange worried glances.

"We'll begin in ten minutes," the proctor said. He looked around the classroom and told them it was their last chance to use the restroom. Albert didn't get up; he was ready to get this over with.

Right before the test began, a girl with bright red pigtails ran into the room and took the last available seat in front of the kid in the Mets jacket. *How could you be late on a day like this?* Albert wondered to himself.

Then from the front of the room, he heard, "Ok, no more talking, kids. The test begins now."

And he was off.

32

Alexa woke up an hour early on her big test day. She was nervous, but more than anything, she was excited. She had a quiet calm about her. She believed that her mother's soul was with her always, but she especially felt it today.

She brushed her teeth, showered, and got dressed in her new purple Billie Eilish sweatshirt over her lucky Jimi Hendrix t-shirt, black jeans, and new Adidas. She even had time to make breakfast for herself before Dad and Celia had gotten up. She was sitting at the kitchen table eating cereal by 6:30 a.m. when she heard her dad's footsteps in the hall.

"Morning, Dad!" she sang out before he had even entered the kitchen.

"Wow, someone's up extra early and ready to go!" he teased her with a smile. "How are you feeling, Alexa?"

"Honestly, Dad, I'm feeling really good about this," she did a little dance in her kitchen chair. "I don't know why, but I'm feeling pretty confident."

"Well, my little Lex Luther, I think you're confident because you're smart, you're hardworking, and you're ready." He walked over to Alexa and gave her a kiss on her forehead.

"Thanks, Dad. I feel ready."

Dad walked over to the cabinet, took down a bowl, and put it on the table. "I'll make myself some coffee and cereal. And why don't you stay right here with your old man until we leave?"

As Alexa handed her dad the almond milk, she thought about the test that could change her life. She knew that if she got in, the only question would be whether she would be comfortable at her new school or feel just as much like an outcast as she did now. Visiting might help give her a clue.

"What time do you want to leave?" Alexa asked. "Oh, and thank you for taking off of work today to take me to the test."

"No problem, kiddo. It's my pleasure. And we don't have to leave here until 7:45, early bird," he answered. "Even if there's crazy traffic."

"No. We should leave at soon as you're done with your cereal," Alexa said with a smile as she put away the almond milk. "Better safe than sorry, like Grandpa Jacob says, right?"

"You're right, sweetheart. We can leave in ten."

They rarely drove into Manhattan. As they approached the corner of Park Avenue and 94th Street, Alexa saw a huge crowd of sixth graders on the block. Some were alone, and some were with parents. It looked like a ton of Asian kids and a handful of other kids. About the only type of kid she didn't see on that block was a kid who looked anything like her.

Alexa was discouraged, but she tried not to let it bother her. "Okay, Dad, you can drop me off here. I'll text you when I get out of the test."

"You sure, hon? I can definitely park and walk you in. You have lots of time, you know!"

"I know, but I'm okay." Her dad pulled over to the side of the curb, and Alexa got out of the car. "Wish me luck!" she said through the car window.

Her dad said back, "You don't need luck, kid! You're the smartest person I know, and I'm so proud of you. But," he smiled and winked at her, "good luck anyway."

Alexa turned on her heels and looked up at the giant brick building. She was in awe. It was bigger than she had imagined. Hunter looked like a fortress. She stood for a moment, staring, before she took a big breath and went inside.

She felt self-conscious being the only Black kid in the building as far as she could tell, but she wouldn't let anything distract her from the task at hand. She got to the front desk and shared her name.

"Welcome, Alexa!" said a cheery, white-haired woman. Alexa couldn't help but smile. "You're early, and I love to see that."

"Hi there." Alexa replied nervously.

"Okay, well, you're in room 202, so you can head on up now if you want to, or you can wait in the lobby, or go get a snack before the exam. You have time."

Alexa didn't want to make herself late, so she headed right up the stairs to room 202. She was one of the first kids there! She decided to sit in the back, so as not to draw any attention to herself . . . though the thought occurred to her that she might draw attention just because of the color of her skin. She really didn't like the thought of that.

A few other kids walked in over the next few minutes. An Asian boy named Albert sat a seat away from her, and a white boy in a Mets jacket sat beside her. The white boy seemed pretty friendly. His name was David. When Albert started talking about his years of tutoring in preparation for the test, Alexa and David shared a concerned glance at each other.

Soon, the room filled up with quiet and anxious kids. Before she knew it, forty minutes had passed, and it was time to take the test. Alexa felt ready.

Suddenly, a girl with bright red hair came flying into the room. With minutes to spare, she took the last seat in the room in the row in front of Alexa. David, the kid in the Mets jacket, congratulated the redhead for making it to the test on time. Alexa tried not to giggle out loud.

Alexa sat eagerly looking at the test booklet, her mind racing. Then she heard, "Okay, no more talking, kids. The test begins now."

She never looked up. Today she would make her mom proud.

33

"So, David," said Mary, the gray-haired therapist who might not have been old, but seemed to David to be wise nonetheless, "how was your week?"

David thought for a moment on that small, comfy couch, as today was supposed to be his final therapy session. It hadn't been a very good week, but he was ready for this to be his final session in therapy, and he was afraid that if he talked about how bad a week it was, he might end up stuck in therapy. He looked up and half-smiled.

"Well," David replied, "it wasn't the best week. But before I tell you about it, I want to let you know that I think I've come a long way, and even if I tell you about a bad week, I still think I'm ready to stop therapy for a while. Is that okay?"

"It's more than okay," said Mary. "It's fantastic. And you *have* come a long way, I totally agree with that. So," she paused and turned her head toward him. "Tell me about your week."

"It's like this," said David sadly. "Things don't really

change. Tony picked on me at school, and my dad is still in the hospital, and I still haven't heard about whether I got into Hunter, and I'm pretty anxious about that. And I'm sad about getting bullied, and really sad about my dad." David looked back down at his lap and closed his eyes for a moment.

"Hmm," said Mary. "It sure does sound like you had a bad week. But I have to disagree with you about something: I think something very big has changed."

"What are you talking about?" David asked. He glanced around her office as if looking for a change there, but there was none to be found: same grandfather clock, same piles of papers and books, same everything.

"When you first came to me, Tony was bullying you, and your dad was sick," Mary said. "But the difference is, you couldn't really talk about your feelings without bursting into tears. It was hard for you to talk about it and identify your feelings. Now, you've just shared some of the same things that are happening to you, but the way you react to them has changed. A lot."

David looked up, then back down at his lap, then back up again with a bit more energy. "Wow. Well, when you put it that way, it does sound like some things have changed," he said with a smile.

"That change is nothing to sneeze at, David," said Mary. "Knowing at age twelve how to identify your feelings, express them, and sit with them calmly and coolly? It's huge. In fact, I know a lot of adults who can't do that as well as you already can."

"Thanks, Mary," said David. "I appreciate it."

"I mean it!" she continued. "In the last several weeks, you've developed some important tools. You can't control your dad and his illness. You can't control a bully like Tony. But you can control how you react, and how you deal with your emotions."

"Got it!" said David. "Okay, I'm feeling pretty good now!"

"Great," said the therapist. "So, let's talk about your anxiety about Hunter. Tell me more."

"Well," David began, "I really want to get in. And I thought we'd hear about it by now. And if I get in it means no more Tony. And . . . I just want to get in! I guess I said that already."

"I understand your anxiety, David!" said Mary. "You really want to get in, and that outcome is really uncertain right now. Let me ask you this: Can you control whether you get in or not at this point?"

"No, of course not," replied David. "I mean, I already took the test, and now, well . . ." David paused there. He realized what Mary was doing. He decided to remain the star student for the day and beat her to the punch.

"Ah, I get it," David revealed. "I can't control whether I get in or not at this point, I can only control how I react to it. So basically, I need to just chill, and know that it will be okay, whether I get in or not . . . even though I *really* want to get in."

David looked at his therapist, eager for her response.

"What you said and how you just said it . . ." said Mary thoughtfully, "you don't need me anymore. At least not right now. I'm so proud of you, David, and how far you've come in therapy. Please keep in touch and let me know how your dad is doing—and of course, let me know when you hear about Hunter."

"I will," said David. "Thanks for everything."

David got up from the chair, put on his Mets jacket, and walked out the door of his therapist's office.

He knew that whether he got into Hunter or not, things were looking up.

34

It was 9:15 p.m., and Tiffany's dad still wasn't home from work.

That can mean only one thing, thought Tiffany.

The question wasn't whether he would come home drunk or not, the question was *when* he'd come home drunk. With her mom already passed out in bed after her long day working at the hospital, Tiffany wanted to make her dad dinner and be the most helpful daughter she could be. But she didn't want to deal with him if he was wasted.

9:30.

9:45.

Tiffany was pretty much out of Instagram stories and TikTok videos to look at. She had long-since finished her homework, and the only thing keeping her up was waiting for her dad.

But Tiffany was getting tired. She was just about ready to call it a night and go to her room when she heard the door being unlocked.

"Tiffany! There you are, my sweetness!" Dad slurred

his words and almost shouted them. He was definitely drunk. "You waited up! Do you have dinner for me? Do yah? Aren't you just the best daughter ever?!"

Tiffany was glad to be considered a good daughter, but it didn't feel very special when he slurred it like that. He almost fell over as he took off his jacket and tried to sit on the couch.

"So have you heard back from your smarty-pants Manhattan school yet, honey?" Dad continued on.

"Hunter, Dad. Hunter. And no. Not yet," Tiffany answered with a sigh. "Getting into Hunter is important to me. I've been working really hard, you know?" She looked down at her feet.

"Oh, don't worry about it! I'm just messing with you, Tiffany!" he slurred. "Why do you have to take everything so see-ree-us-a-lee? You're just a kid." He stuck out his tongue at her like a child.

Tiffany wished she could feel sorry for her drunk dad, but she couldn't. She was angry! Not only had she waited up for him, but she had made dinner for him. And the way he repaid her was to come home drunk, and then tease her about something that was important to her.

"Why can't you *ever* take anything except for drinking see-ree-us-a-lee, Dad?" Tiffany said, mocking him.

"What? What did you say?" Dad's red eyes glistened in the light of the TV. His voice was low, and she smelled tequila on his breath. Tiffany could tell his blood was beginning to boil as he rubbed his forehead. Dad's temper came on quickly, and as he moved toward her, Tiffany flinched. Drunk Dad was usually harmless, but occasionally Angry Drunk Dad came out, and he could be terrifying.

"Nothing, nothing, Dad. Forget it," Tiffany grumbled, moving backward. But it was too late.

"No, I won't forget it, young lady," he barked, his voice getting louder and sloppier as he continued. "I heard you, and I think you're a rude, spoiled girl. Your sister doesn't talk back to me, and your mother doesn't talk back to me like that."

"Are you kidding me right now?!" Tiffany yelled back at him. She took a step toward him and continued, like a fire was suddenly burning inside of her. "How could they talk back to you? Julie is never home, and Mom just acts like everything is normal, and that you're not out at the bar every night!" She paused, watching him. He just stared and swayed on his feet. She couldn't stop now. "Spoiled? I make dinner almost every night of the week *and* I clean the house! I get straight A's, I'm never in trouble at school . . . " She buried her head in her hands. "How could you call me rude? Spoiled?" She began to weep.

Her dad seemed as surprised as Tiffany by the words coming out of her mouth. His eyes had grown wide, and he had stepped back, but now his eyes narrowed again. "You know what I bet they like at that stupid school you want to go to," he spat, "I mean, this 'smart' school of yours? I bet they like . . . I bet they like . . . I bet they like girls with manners. Manners, Tiffany Beth . . ."

He sat suddenly on the couch behind him. His head nodded back and then forward again, and his eyes began to close. He raised up his hand, but it fell back onto his lap.

And just like that, he was asleep.

Tiffany was stunned. She didn't know what had come over her, and now she just wanted to go to bed and forget about this whole night. She looked at her dad, fast asleep. *He probably won't even remember this,* she thought. She went and grabbed a blanket from the closet, then covered him with it. He was already snoring.

She walked to the kitchen to cover his dinner and put it in the fridge. On her way out of the kitchen, she stopped and looked at her dad for a long time. Then she walked over and kissed him on the cheek and whispered, "Goodnight, Dad."

She was in bed soon after, but she didn't fall asleep quickly. She was up most of the night thinking about the Hunter test, and her dad, and her mom. It was all so . . . complicated. Why couldn't her family just be normal? But she knew that while she wanted the best for her parents, she needed the best for herself. And that meant the best education she could possibly get.

She closed her eyes and finally fell asleep.

35

Albert had never seen his mom so stressed out. She cleaned constantly, spoke faster and more than usual, and when she didn't do those things, she paced around their apartment. Albert felt like he could see her heart beating out of her chest every time he looked at her. You would have thought she was waiting to find out if she was going to live or die!

Of course, she wasn't. She was just waiting to find out whether Albert got into Hunter or not.

When she was stressed, she cleaned obsessively. By the time it got to a snowy Thursday evening in February, Albert's apartment was immaculate.

"Albert!" screamed Mom as he walked in the door after school. "Did you wipe your boots on the mat outside the door?"

"Yes, Mom," sighed Albert, tired after a long day. He walked into the small kitchen and took a seat at the table next to her.

"Good. Thank you, Albert," uttered Mom. "How was

your day at school? I got home early to clean up and to make you some soup. Would you like some? You could sure use some soup, right?"

"Sure, Mom," Albert replied. "I'll take some soup. And school was fine. And after-school group tutoring was fine too."

"Well," continued Mom, "what did you hear about Hunter at after-school? They should have the inside scoop on when families will find out if they got in or not." She placed a large bowl of chicken soup with dumplings and a spoon on the table. Steam rose from the top, and shiny round dumplings bobbed up and down in the broth.

Albert blew on the soup and picked up his spoon. "I don't know, Mom," said Albert. "Don't you think if I knew I would tell you?" Albert froze for a moment, staring at his soup. He realized he shouldn't have said that. He quickly added, "By the way, Mom, the soup looks great! Thank you so much. Nothing beats your cooking."

He looked up to smile at her. But it was too late.

"Don't you get fresh with me, young man," said his mother, raising her brows and slowing her speech. She got louder. "I don't work twelve hours a day, six days a week, and send you to an after-school tutoring program so you can learn the wrong habits from all these American boys and talk to your mother like that."

"Sorry, Mom," said Albert. And he really was. But he knew with Mom stressed out to start with, this wasn't going to go away so quickly.

"Does Paul talk to his mom like that?"

"No, Mom."

"Well, do you talk to your father like that?"

"No, Mom."

"Wait a minute!" she said. "You talk to me like that and show no respect to your mother, but you don't talk to your father like that?"

Albert swallowed and stared at her. "I'm so sorry, Mom," he promised. "I was very disrespectful." He put his head down in shame.

"Yes, you were. Now answer my question!"

"No, I don't talk to my father like that. And I shouldn't talk to you like that, either." Albert looked to the left and right in desperation, thinking of some way to change the subject. He decided to try a teeny, little lie to get out of this one. "Mom, guess what? They said at after-school that the Hunter test results should be coming in the next couple of days!"

"Really?" Mom perked up. "Tomorrow, or in two days?

"Two days, I think," Albert said. The truth was, he *had* heard this, but it wasn't from his instructor, it was from Paul. Still, he wasn't *technically* lying.

"Oh, good," said his mom. She smiled and looked out the window. "I have a good feeling about it, but, of course, I don't want to jinx it. I'm glad you like the soup, son."

Phew! thought Albert. He had escaped from his mom's wrath. Now he just needed an acceptance letter to fly his way in two days, and all would be good.

"It's great, Mom! Love you."

He got up from the table and gave his mom a longer hug than usual.

Albert skipped away to his room, full of hope . . . and soup.

36

Alexa was on her way to get a snack one night when she clearly heard her name being spoken in the kitchen. Alexa stopped. It was Celia and Dad. Alexa didn't mean to eavesdrop, but Celia was so loud, Alexa couldn't *help* but hear her. Alexa edged closer to the kitchen on her tippy-toes so nobody would hear her.

"Do you think Alexa should go to Hunter if she gets in?" Celia said clearly. "She's had so much trouble fitting in at the school she's been in her whole life. I hope she'll be able to make new friends there. I worry about her. And no matter what I do, she is just not warming up to me, James."

When her dad answered, he sounded tired. "Of course she's going to go to Hunter. It's one of the best schools in the country," he replied. "If she gets in, it's like winning the lottery! And as for friends, well, she has Laura. It's quality over quantity, right?" He chuckled, then paused. "It's really important to her. And it's helping her stay connected to her mother."

"I know," Celia said, her voice lowered, "I just don't want her to be in over her head. It's been a tough few years for her already. Our getting married so quickly wasn't exactly easy on her either."

Alexa now stood inches from the swinging door into the kitchen. *That's it!* thought Alexa, annoyed. She didn't want Celia talking about her, wondering what was best for her! *You're not my mom!* ran through Alexa's mind over and over again. She wanted their conversation to be over, but she didn't want them to know she had been listening.

Alexa took ten big, quiet steps backward, away from the door. Then she shouted, "Dad! Celia! I'm hungry for a snack. Do we have anything good in the house?" Then she walked loudly toward the kitchen and swung open the door.

"Oh, hi, guys!" she said a little too cheerfully as she slid through the door. "What's going on?"

Her dad answered honestly, much to Alexa's surprise. "We were actually just talking about whether or not you should go if you get into Hunter," he said.

Alexa was glad she didn't have to hide her frustration, because it was bubbling out of her. "You mean *when* I get in right? And I thought we talked about this, Dad. When I get in, I'm going! Why wouldn't I?"

Her dad shook his head. "Whoa, I—I didn't say you wouldn't go. I just said we were talking about it," he said. "In fact, why don't we cross that bridge when we come to it?" Her dad smiled at Alexa and grabbed a bag from the counter behind him. "Oh! I bought you Utz BBQ potato chips on my way home." He shook the bag in front of Alexa. "Your favorite!"

Alexa didn't smile. She turned away from the chips her dad was dangling between them and instead looked at Celia. "What do you think, Celia?" she pried. "You've been pretty quiet since I walked in."

"I'm not sure what I think," Celia said, and took a sip of her red wine. "I know that you're a smart girl, and that everything will work out the way it's supposed to, right?"

"Yep, it will," Alexa said.

The conversation about Hunter seemed to be over. Alexa broke down and opened the bag of chips, and her dad started talking about a new project at his work.

But after a few minutes, Alexa didn't feel well. She asked her dad if she could talk to him in the living room.

"Sure, hon." He motioned to Alexa to step outside the kitchen.

They walked to the living room and sat down on their velvety, green couch. Her dad looked into her big, brown eyes and asked softly, "What's the matter, Al?"

Alexa looked down at her hands. "When will I stop missing Mom?" she asked, fighting back tears.

Her dad sighed. "I don't think ever, Alexa. I know I'll always miss her."

"It's not fair," she trembled. "And I'm trying so hard to like Celia, I am, but she just makes me miss Mommy even more. And she'll never be Mommy, ever!"

"I know, Alexa. I know." He put his arm around her. "She's trying. We're all trying. Celia really does care for you, and this is all very new to her too. It's going to take some time. I know you're stressed about school, and it's all hard. But you know what?" His voice was still soft.

"What?" Alexa asked.

"Like I told you before: it's all going to be okay. I mean it."

Alexa kind of knew it too, but it didn't take away from how much she missed her mom, how badly she wanted to go to Hunter, and her constant anger at Celia for butting into their lives.

"Dad? If I get in, I have to go to Hunter. I just have to go. I know Mom would have wanted it. I just absolutely know it."

"I know, sweetheart, I know." Dad hugged her tight, and she could feel him crying.

Alexa realized that her dad was still hurting too. She knew he would never do anything to hurt her. She thought about that while her dad was still hugging her and crying softly. Her mom would have wanted her dad to be happy. So maybe she *could* give Celia a second chance, for her dad's sake. Maybe she could let go of her anger for Celia. She realized that she was already feeling a little better.

A few weeks later, Alexa got home on a cold, wintry Tuesday a little later than usual, since she'd stayed after school to work on her science project. She was feeling stressed, especially since Natasha and her crew still wouldn't leave her alone. Every day they made fun of her for something; her love of wearing purple, her love of math . . . she even had to ask Celia not to pick her up in front of her school anymore. Natasha and her girls were straight up mean and relentless. She just wanted to go to her room and veg out for a while.

So, when Alexa walked through the door at 5:30 p.m. to find her dad and Celia already home and waiting for her, it was both strange and annoying.

They were sitting on the couch, staring at her. Her dad was grinning ear to ear. "Welcome home, Alexa!" he said as soon as she managed to close the front door behind her. "I made your favorite spaghetti and meatballs for dinner."

"Awesome, thanks," Alexa said, surprised but weary. She was tired.

"Come sit down. We have something to talk about." Dad was acting weird. He patted the couch cushion next to him.

"Okay . . ." Alexa said nervously. "Let me just put down my things and go to the bathroom. Can you please give me, like, five minutes?" Alexa headed toward her room.

"Of course," Dad called after her.

Alexa wasn't sure if this was going to be good news or bad news, but something big was going to be discussed. She put down her backpack and headed to the bathroom. Then she headed toward the kitchen for some spaghetti and meatballs.

Celia started serving the food while her dad began

slowly, "Alexa, we've got some pretty big news. Are you ready?"

"Okay . . . sure," Alexa answered.

Dad continued: "Okay, so, we got the mail today," and he held up an envelope.

Of course! thought Alexa. *The Hunter test results!* How could she have forgotten?

"You got into Hunter!" he said, as Celia came around the table to give Alexa a hug.

Alexa's breath was taken away. She felt overwhelmed with joy. She took the letter from her dad and read it a few times, making sure it was real.

A few minutes passed as everyone started in on their piles of dad's spaghetti. Then Alexa's dad began to speak, "So, Alexa, that was the good news," Dad said. "But there is some not-so-great news as well."

Alexa's smile fell, and she opened her mouth to speak, but Dad put his hand up. "Okay, let me finish. To be honest, Alexa, I've been doing a lot of research, and Hunter is even less racially diverse than we had hoped. Less than five percent of the student body is Black, and less than two percent of that are girls. And that's really not wonderful." He paused and glanced at Celia. After a moment, he continued. "So, here's the deal: Hunter is one of the best schools in the country, and if you want to go, well . . . I won't stop you."

Alexa couldn't hold her emotions back now. "Oh, thank you!" she shouted. "I'm so—"

"Now, wait a minute," her dad interjected. "This means two things: one, you are still going to have to take part in church activities on the weekends, which means your schedule is going to be tight; and second, you'd better be prepared to have a father who is very active in the PTA, helping to change the game at your new school. Because a school for the smartest kids in New York City with no Black girls. . . . Ain't nobody got time for that!"

When her father was done, Alexa was quiet. She thought about how overwhelming it had been the day she took the test and saw zero Black kids there. She didn't like that. But she also didn't like getting bullied at her neighborhood school. And she knew, more than anything else in the world, that her mom would have wanted her to go to Hunter. She imagined her mom there at the table, telling Alexa that she was so proud of her, telling her to be brave.

"You look deep in thought, Alexa," her dad said, bringing Alexa back to reality. "What are you thinking? Celia and I are really proud of you, you know. And we think this is an amazing opportunity for you. And we know you're going to work hard and keep your grades up."

"Ha!" Alexa laughed out loud. "Obvi! And yes! I'm in. I'm going! Thank you, Dad. Thank you, Celia."

Celia pointed her fork toward Alexa. "This is going to be a great thing, Alexa. Now eat those meatballs before they get cold! Your father worked on them for over an hour!"

Alexa dug into her dinner and smiled. She appreciated

that her dad was looking out for her, even if he was a little intense sometimes. Then, slowly, her smile fell, and a tear ran down her cheek.

"What's the matter, Alexa?" asked Dad. "Your old man's spaghetti is that bad, eh?"

Alexa laughed through her tears. "No, silly," she said. "I was just thinking about Mom. I think she'd be proud of me too."

"Look at me," her dad said. "I *know* she'd be proud of you. In fact, I know she *is* proud of you today, smiling down on you from Heaven. She asked you to work hard at school and get good grades, and look at you now! Just incredible. Isn't that right, Celia?"

"That's one hundred percent right. She is proud of you, Alexa. And so are we."

Alexa finished her dinner and asked if she could eat her ice cream in her room. She had to text Laura and tell her the great news!

37

David had a strange feeling today would be the day he found out if he got into Hunter. For one thing, he had emailed the Admissions office, and they told him that letters had gone out two days before. (*Letters?* thought David. *Who sent physical letters anymore?*)

More importantly, David had found a few people on Instagram who had received their letters and had gotten in. David didn't know any of them, but he had been searching hashtags on Instagram and found two boys and one girl who had posted pics of their acceptance letters.

Unfortunately, the mail in Sunset Park, Brooklyn was often late. So, on this Thursday afternoon in February, David sat in his room, alone, staring past his Mets poster out the window, waiting for the mailman to come. The mail was supposed to be there by 4:00 p.m., but it was 5:30, and still no mail!

David was thinking of giving up when he saw the mailman approaching. David hopped up out of his seat faster than ever before, ran downstairs, and met the man at the front door before he had time to put the mail in the mail slot.

"Thanks, I'll take that!" David shouted with a harried smile. David grabbed the stack of mail and sorted through it hurriedly: bill, bill, catalog, bill, bill, catalog, catalog. *Why do stores send so many catalogs?* David screamed in his head. He passed over one more bill and then he saw it: an envelope with a purple Hunter symbol on it.

This was it. It was addressed to "Parents of David Kaplan," so he wasn't sure if he should open it. David hesitated for a moment, then tore up the envelope and unfolded the letter:

"Dear Parents of David Kaplan: We are pleased to accept your child, David Kaplan, for enrollment into Hunter High School, beginning in September."

There was more, but David stopped reading. He did a fist pump and hopped up in the air.

"Mom! Mom! I got in!" he shouted as he ran through the kitchen and living room to find her. "I can't believe it! I actually got in!"

"That's great!" said Mom, rushing out from her bedroom to hug David. "Where did you get in?" she asked.

David stepped back to look at her. *What?* he thought. It seemed totally unfathomable that she wouldn't know exactly what he was talking about, given how much this meant to him—and more importantly how much he had been talking about it almost every day. Maybe she was joking? But she didn't look like she was joking. David shook his head.

"Hunter, Mom. Hunter. I got into Hunter!"

"Oh, right! That's wonderful, David," she replied. "I'm so proud of you."

David was still in shock for a moment after that. But he figured she had been so distracted with Dad and his mental illness lately, he could forgive her. Plus, his excitement was pushing out any other feelings right now.

"Thanks. I'm proud of myself, actually!" David smiled ear-to-ear. "I'm going to map out a new route to get to school, I think. I found another subway route that I think will save me ten minutes, and I have lots of time to practice this summer, and—"

"David, hon," Mom interrupted. "I'm so sorry to stop you and I'm so excited for you, really I am, but I just need to call this psychiatrist back about your dad changing his meds. Let's celebrate later, okay?"

David dropped his shoulders and looked down at his feet. "Sure," he said. "We can celebrate later."

Mom lifted David's face up to meet hers. "Maybe pizza? Extra cheese?" she pleaded with a half-smile.

"Sure. Pizza's great. Thanks," David answered, smiling but not doing a very good job of it.

"Great, I'll order soon. Congrats again, David! And one more thing?"

"Sure. What's up, Mom?" David asked.

"Can you please watch your brother and sister for a

little while? They're watching TV, so it should be easy."
She kissed his head. "That's my boy!" Mom nodded in
approval and then was gone, back to her room to call the
psychiatrist.

"Sure," said David.

He sat down and put his head in his lap. But then he
looked up and smiled to himself.

He would be going Hunter in the fall, and nothing
could change that.

38

Tiffany knew that if she got into Hunter, it wasn't a done deal. She had a feeling that even though her parents had let her take the test, and even though they had said she could go if she got in, it wouldn't be so simple.

And she was about to find out if she was right, because she was staring right at her acceptance letter. Mom, Dad, and her sister were all out, like usual, and she was home alone with the mail. Her first thought was happiness and excitement. It felt good to be told you were smart and special. Her second thought was, *Should I text Mom and Dad?*

On the one hand, she wanted to share the news with them. On the other hand, she wanted to see their reactions in person, and to be ready to discuss it with them if they weren't both happy like she was.

She decided to wait. And she decided not to tell anyone about getting into Hunter before she told her parents.

Now, the question was: how long would she be waiting? Mom was usually home between 6 p.m. and 7 p.m. Dad, well, he could be home before Mom, but if he went out drinking, he could be home at midnight or later.

Tiffany had to optimize her chances of getting the news to them tonight, so she group-texted them along with her sister, Julie: *Have some news. Cooking steak. Does 7 p.m. work for all of you?*

Mom texted back right away: *Yes, thank you, hon.*

Dad texted back a few minutes later: *Yup, I'll be there. Can't wait!*

Julie texted back expectedly: *Sorry, I have a date. Hope this news is good! XOXO*

Okay, two out of three wasn't bad—plus, it was the two who actually mattered. Tiffany began preparing a steak, seasoning it just the way she knew her dad liked it. She preheated the oven. She wanted dinner to be ready by 7:15 p.m., in case one of her parents was late. She set the table beautifully.

7 p.m. finally rolled around. "Hello, angel!" called out her mom as she walked in the door. "What a day I've had! I'm so happy to be home, and wow! That table looks gorgeous, like you! Give me five minutes to change."

She walked over to Tiffany, kissed her on the cheek, and went to her bedroom.

Now it was up to Dad. The bad news was, he wasn't home. The good news was, Tiffany got a text from him right away: *Stuck in traffic, be home soon. XO*

Oh, man, thought Tiffany. *Stuck in traffic or stuck at a bar?*

She refused to get her hopes up. *Whatever will be, will be,* she thought. But it wasn't easy. With every minute that went by, Tiffany got more and more anxious. It wasn't fair that she always had to worry about when and if Dad would be home.

Mom came down ten minutes later. The steak was fully cooked and ready to go. "So, what's your news, Tiff?" Mom asked as she sat down at the table.

Tiffany chewed on her bottom lip. "Do you think Dad will be home soon?" she asked.

"You know Dad!" Mom smiled and rolled her eyes, both explaining and forgiving him in one short statement.

Yup, I know Dad, Tiffany thought. She wanted to say, "I know that he's a drunk and he's probably not coming home 'til late. What else is new?" But she just couldn't say it out loud.

"Yup. Sure do," she said instead. "Should we start the steak without him?"

"Let's wait a bit more. This table really does look bea-u-ti-ful!" Mom smiled and poured herself a glass of wine.

At 7:28, Dad walked in.

"Hi! Sorry I'm a little late. Steak time!" he announced on his way through the kitchen door.

He smiled at Tiffany, and she couldn't help but smile back. The three of them sat down to dinner.

"This steak is delicious! You've outdone yourself, Tiffany," her dad said after his first bite, wiping his face with a napkin. He had never mentioned the night that

Tiffany yelled at him—either he was avoiding it, or he didn't remember. Either way worked for Tiffany.

Mom added, "I have to say, he's right. Nice job, Tiff. Now, what was that news?"

"Well," Tiffany said, putting down her fork and pausing for a breath, "you remember that test I took to get into that school, Hunter? I got in!" The rest she said very quickly: "I know you wanted me to go to the same schools you went to, Mom, but I really, really want to go! This means so much to me, and I promise to work super hard if you let me go, and—"

Mom interrupted: "Okay, okay." She looked at Tiffany's dad, who smiled and shrugged at her mom. Mom continued, "I did think you were going to go to my high school. I still don't see anything wrong with it. But"—she looked straight at Tiffany—"it is a very good school, and if you keep up the hard work, and if you can cook us up a steak like this every so often, it's okay by us." Her mom winked at her.

Tiffany was ecstatic. "Thank you, thank you, thank you!" she shouted and jumped out of her seat to kiss her mom on the cheek first and then her dad. She did a victory lap around the kitchen table and quickly returned to her steak.

She had no idea what she was in for, but for now, she sure was happy.

39

Albert's mom never took off from work. She never went on vacation and she never called in sick. She never arrived late to anything, and she never ever left early. The fact that she had left the office at 3 p.m. that day in order to be home when Albert got the mail . . . well, that was a *huge* deal.

Word had gotten out in the Chinatown community that today was the day that Hunter letters would be received— and Albert's mom was going to be there when he opened up that letter.

While Albert's mom cooked and cleaned the kitchen, Albert sat at the kitchen table, texting in a group chat with sixteen kids from his after-school tutoring group. So far, only three of them had gotten the mail today, and unfortunately, none of the three had been accepted. That was not a good sign. Albert tapped the kitchen table with his fingers. A few seconds later, his phone chimed again.

"Is that my phone?" Mom shrieked. She franticly dug in her pocket.

"No, Mom, it wasn't," Albert assured her. "It was my

phone. Calm down. I'll go downstairs and check the mail again before dinner."

Mom stood tall, her shoulders back and her head held high. "I asked Mrs. Zhang at the shop downstairs to text me when the mailman came today."

"I guess you're really looking forward to getting the mail today," Albert replied with a soft smile.

"Albert, you know what today is," she said as she sat next to him. "The truth is, I am proud of you no matter what. But I think we both know how much this means if you get in." Mom started talking faster and faster. "You can go to Hunter, then Harvard, then become a doctor or, if you prefer, an engineer. Either way—"

Mom's phone buzzed. She read the message and her head sprang up.

Albert sat frozen in his seat until Mom said, "Go! Go get the mail!"

Albert got up and darted out the door and down the stairs to the mailbox. He opened it and took everything out. In the middle of the stack of mail, there was an envelope from Hunter. He took a deep breath, ran back up to the third floor, and went back inside the apartment. He put down the mail on the table and handed the Hunter envelope to his mom.

"You open it, Albert. I'm too nervous." Mom's brow was furrowed, and her jaw was clenched.

Albert was nervous too. This moment meant a lot to him, but more importantly, he knew how much this meant to his mom. In fact, it seemed like she had been waiting all of *her* life for this moment in *his* life. That was an awful lot of pressure. He took a deep breath in, tore open the letter, and stared at the first page.

"Albert?!" Mom shouted within two seconds.

"Yes, I got in, Mom!" Albert shouted back. "I got in! I got in!"

Albert's mom started crying immediately. She looked up at the ceiling and mouthed something in Chinese. Then Albert, who never cried, burst into tears.

"I'm so proud of you, son!" Mom said as she wiped the tears off her cheeks. "So proud of you. I'm calling your father. You can check in with your friends."

Albert allowed himself to smile as fully as he could ever remember doing. As great as it felt to get in, he had to admit he felt extra joy when his mom said she was going to call his dad. That hadn't happened in a good way in a long time.

Albert listened in as his mom called his dad, excitedly telling him that he had gotten into Hunter. Then he grabbed his iPhone and posted in the group chat that he had gotten in. He scrolled up to see the messages he had missed in those few minutes: three other kids from his class had gotten in. He didn't really talk to any of them much. No word from Paul yet. How great would it be if he and his best friend went to Hunter together?

Just then, he got a notification of a new text—from Paul!

It wasn't in the group chat; it was an individual text. *I didn't get in, man. SUX. Sorry bro.*

Albert shook his head. *I'm so sorry, brother. Screw them!* he texted back.

It was bittersweet: his best friend didn't get in, but he couldn't help but think that now he would get a fresh start in the fall, at a school where nobody knew his family secret.

He put down his phone and ran over to his mom, who was now standing across the room, smiling at him. He gave her a big hug, and it seemed like she never wanted to let go.

40

June and July flew by for David. Tony and his crew still bullied him right up until the last day of school in June, but David didn't care as much anymore. He knew he was headed for Hunter.

July brought David lots of free time. He spent most of it playing Among Us with his brother and sister. His family spent a couple of super-hot days at the neighborhood pool in Sunset Park. It was crowded, but fun.

Best of all, it seemed like his dad was doing well and regulating his mood, and Mom seemed to be handling everything smoothly.

August was another story.

It was hot in New York—like, uncomfortably hot, the kind of hot where you wake up sweating in the morning and go to sleep sweating at night—and for some reason David couldn't understand, his dad decided to stop taking his meds for his bipolar disorder that month. Within just a few days, he had gone pretty mad again. David walked in on him in the bathroom, on a Friday afternoon, shaving his head and singing the old Billy Joel song "We Didn't Start the Fire" to himself.

David stared at his dad in disbelief. Why was this happening again? He knew immediately his dad was sick and needed to go back to a psych ward right away. He texted his mom at work and then promptly called 9-1-1. "I . . . I need help. My dad's not well," he stammered out before sharing his address.

Luckily, his brother and sister were downstairs playing video games, and he hoped it would stay that way for a while. Mom couldn't get home in time, so when two police officers arrived, David escorted them to the bathroom himself.

One officer said to Dad, "Hello, sir. Can you please identify yourself?"

Dad replied, "I'm Jesus H. Christ, and I'm here to save you."

David felt both sad and embarrassed, watching the scene unfold in front of him. It took every ounce of self-control he had not to start crying, but he had to be strong.

"Where's your mom?" the officer asked. He was tall, with a mustache and dark brown hair. He had a warm smile.

"She's working. She'll be home soon," David replied. His dad kept singing "We Didn't Start the Fire," and the police officers just stared at him. The tall one turned to the other and whispered, "What the heck are we going to do with this one?" The shorter, female officer shrugged.

"He has to be a threat to himself or to you kids for us to do something, is the thing," said the male cop. The female cop just stood there looking half-amused and half-scared herself.

David looked at his father, nearly bald by now, repeating the song over and over in the mirror. "Dad, I'm scared," pleaded David. "I want you to get some help."

His dad suddenly jumped farther into the bathroom and stared wildly at David and the cops. "Stand back, or I'll shoot!" Dad shouted, and he held up the razor toward them.

That was enough for the cops. The male cop picked up his phone and dialed. "I need an ambulance over to my location, stat," he said. "Code 252. Bring a strait jacket in case he fights us."

David tried hard to hold it together. This wasn't the first time Dad had been taken away in an ambulance to the psych ward, but it was the first time it had happened while his mom wasn't home. And it was absolutely terrifying. He thought about what he had learned in therapy, and he took a deep breath. With the cops watching Dad, David walked to the kitchen faucet and poured himself a glass of water. He took a sip and one more deep breath.

The female officer walked into the kitchen. "What time is your mom going to be home, kid?" she asked. "Because we can't leave you kids alone in the house. She needs to be back here soon, or we're going to have to take you with us to the station."

That was enough for David to completely lose it. He started crying and blurted out, "But I haven't done anything! We haven't done anything wrong! *Why*?!"

"You're not being arrested, kid. We just need to make sure you're safe."

David had already dialed his mom. "When are you going to be home? I need you home now."

"I'm walking in the house right now," she answered. David instantaneously turned around and almost laughed with relief.

"I'm here. I'm right here!" Mom called, out of breath as she came through the door.

"Mrs. Kaplan! Great, you're here," said the male officer when Mom arrived at the bathroom door. "We're going to take your husband in a few minutes, okay? Can you stay with your kids?"

"Yes, sure, officer. Thank you," she said. She turned to David, put her hand on the side of his face, and said, "Thank you, David, for dealing with this while I was out." She kissed his forehead and quietly asked him, "Can you can go downstairs and check on Philip and Dani, please?"

"Of course, Mom."

"Bye, Dad," David said, relieved to escape the situation for now, but sad and scared and overwhelmed by it all, nonetheless.

"Goodbye, my son," his dad sang out. "The child is the father of the man."

David turned, put his head down, and walked away.

Once in the kitchen, he saw a note in the mail from Hunter on the counter: it was his schedule for the fall. *Can't wait to get out of here and spend my days there,* he thought.

Luckily for David, that was only a few weeks away.

41

Tiffany's summer was going by fast. She spent her days at the YMCA camp in Queens; they did fun things and went on a lot of field trips. And most weekends, she went to the beach with her family.

It was weird: for most of the year, she felt like she barely saw her parents or her sister. But when summer rolled around, they spent a lot more time together. It was as if somehow, when the calendar hit July, they became a *normal* family.

Every Saturday, Tiffany's mom woke up early and dragged everyone else out of bed, and the four of them headed to Rockaway Beach for the day. The girls would play in the sand when they were younger, but now they all just lay out on the beach. Tiffany and her mom usually had a book to read, her sister was either on her phone or sleeping, and Dad . . .well, Dad brought two six-packs of beer and drank until he passed out in the sun. Dad always drove them to the beach in the morning, and Mom drove home in the evening.

It was a family tradition, and no matter what, it brought them together.

This particular Saturday in August started off the usual way: Mom woke up early and got everyone else up, and they packed up the car to head to the beach. It actually started off better than usual, because Tiffany had gotten an orientation packet from Hunter the day before with her schedule and a bunch of other materials from her new school.

Once they had settled into their spot on the beach, Tiffany pulled out her schedule. "Mom, Dad, check out my schedule from Hunter," Tiffany urged them. She looked up from her packet with her sunglasses on. "In addition to the usual math, science, English, social studies stuff, I have a class called Communications and Theater. This says it's mandatory for all seventh graders to take, and I'll learn about public speaking and communications and stuff."

"That sounds interesting, Tiffany," Mom said as she stretched out across her beach towel. "Actually, it sounds a lot more valuable than most classes in school!" She turned to Dad. "Doesn't it, hon?"

Dad put down his beer, pulled out a flask from his pocket, and took a sip of something that Tiffany knew wasn't beer . . . or water.

"My schedule is changing too," he muttered. "Maybe I should take Communications and Theater."

"What does that mean?" Mom scowled at him.

"I got laid off from work yesterday, that's what I

mean," he grumbled. He took another sip from the flask, then set it down on the ground. He turned to Mom and sighed. "Sorry I didn't tell you earlier. I was embarrassed, all right?"

Mom pursed her lips, then looked at Tiffany and relaxed them. She turned back to Dad. "I'm so sorry, honey," she assured him. "It's okay. We'll get through it." She seemed surprisingly fine. Tiffany wasn't so sure she believed her.

"I'm sorry to hear that, Dad," Tiffany said, genuinely concerned. "Hey, what's in the flask?"

"None of your business, that's what's in the flask!" Dad shouted back at her and took another gulp. He had already had three beers and a lot of whatever was in that flask, and it wasn't even noon yet.

"Dad, I can use the internet to help you find another job," suggested Tiffany, trying again. "I know about LinkedIn, and Indeed, and all these sites."

"Don't worry about me, Tiffany," her dad snapped back. "I'll be fine. The last thing I need is my kids worried about finding me a job. Now let's change the subject. Tell me more about that schedule of yours." He took another chug from the flask.

Tiffany frowned. She put her schedule in her bag and quickly got up. "Actually, I think I'm going to go for a swim," she said and pointed at the ocean. "Mom, Jules, want to come?"

Both Julie and Mom shook their heads. *Just like them*

to put their heads in the sand and pretend there's no pro-blem, she thought. But all she said out loud was, "Okay, see ya!"

Tiffany went for a long swim followed by a long walk on the beach. She had to get away and think for a bit. She was concerned: about Dad losing his job, about Dad's drinking, about Mom never really paying attention. She was scared of what might happen to her dad and to her family sooner or later. She wished she could talk to her mom about the fight she'd had with her dad, but she knew that she couldn't. In the Russo house there were rules, and two of them were: 1) Do *not* talk back to your parents, and 2) Adult business is just that—for adults. Stirring the pot now would just cause more tension in an already uncom-fortable situation.

By the time she got back to her family's spot on the beach, it was 3:30. Mom was sitting up, checking her phone. Her face had a worried look on it, but when she turned and saw Tiffany approaching, she let out a sigh of relief. "Well, that was a long swim! I was beginning to get worried!" Mom smiled big, but her voice was a bit shaky.

"Sorry, I went for a walk too," Tiffany said.

"It's okay," Mom said, "but we should get going home." She turned and tapped Dad's shoulder. "Gino, time to wake up! We're heading home!" Mom shook him a bit, but Dad didn't respond.

"Dad!" Tiffany and Julie both yelled together. This wasn't the first time Dad had passed out after drinking beers all day in the heat at the beach, but he usually responded when they shook him.

Mom got up and walked over to where half of Dad's face was in the sand. She knelt in front of him. Her nostrils flared as she shook him again, harder. She reached over him, grabbed a bottle of water off of his towel, and dumped it on his face. But Dad wasn't budging.

Mom shut her eyes, tightened her mouth to a scowl, and stood up. "He's still breathing," she said. She stood with her hands on her hips, looking down at him. "I think he's going to have to sleep this one off." She turned to Tiffany and Julie, who were both standing with their towels and bags in their hands. "Let's go," Mom said. "Your father can Uber home when he wakes up."

Tiffany couldn't believe it. Mom was going to leave Dad at the beach. "Are you sure, Mom?" asked Tiffany.

Her mom sighed, then held her head high. "I'm sure," she promised. "His drinking, his problem. Come on."

Tiffany was stunned. That was the first time her mom had said anything about her dad's drinking. Tiffany felt a wave of emotions: relief, fear, sadness . . . and a part of her was happy. Maybe she could talk to her mom about her dad's drinking now, about all the ways it made her feel.

Before they headed home, Tiffany checked her dad's cell phone to make sure it was charged and texted him: *Love you, Dad. XOXO*

She didn't really know what else to say.

They turned to walk toward the car. Once everything

was packed, Tiffany sat in the back seat. She turned to look back through the rear window, but couldn't pick out her dad in the sea of people on the sand.

42

Albert was having a really fun summer. He had math and science camp every Monday through Thursday morning, but that was actually more fun than school, and Paul was in camp with him.

Then every afternoon he would hang out with his friends, or go to a movie, or hang around the house. His mom wanted him to study, but she genuinely seemed okay with him slacking off a bit after working so hard for so many years in school.

Weekends were the best, though. Dad and Guillermo took him on adventures almost every weekend, most of them three-day weekends starting on Fridays. They went to upstate New York, to Hershey Park in Philadelphia, and to Washington, D.C. Guillermo was always looking for a new adventure for them to experience, and he really brought out the fun and adventure in Dad. Before Guillermo, Dad always had seemed . . . well . . . boring. But now he was so much fun to be around.

Even better than weekends, though, was that Mom

and Dad were getting along better than Albert had seen in a long time. Obviously, they were never going to get back together, but they were friendlier and more accepting of one another. She no longer referred to him as "that Guillermo" and had stopped wincing when Guillermo appeared at the door with Dad in his bright pastel shirt. Albert was very grateful for that.

Yup, all was going well until the last weekend in August, when Dad, Guillermo, and Albert returned home from a weekend in Vermont.

Albert should have suspected something when Guillermo came upstairs with them for drop-off. He never came upstairs with them.

"Shuchun," said Dad when she came out to greet them, "can we talk for a minute?"

"Of course, Bob," said Mom. "Privately?"

"Yes please," replied Dad. Albert knew that meant "without Albert," since Guillermo was obviously there for the conversation.

"Albert, can you please go to your room so your mother and father can talk for a minute?" asked Mom.

Albert went to his room, but in their small apartment, with his ear to the wall, and his dad's loud voice, he could basically hear the whole conversation anyway.

"Shuchun," his dad was saying, "I wanted to let you know that I'm thinking of joining the NQAPIA. It's the leading organization for gay Asians."

"Okay, congratulations!" said Mom. "Why do I care?"

"Well, the reason I'm telling you now, Shuchun," Dad continued, "is that we may march in the Pride parade coming up."

"*What*?!" shrieked Mom. "What if people see you?"

"That's exactly why I thought it was the right thing to do to tell you in advance," said Dad calmly, almost too quietly for Albert to hear.

"I was just getting used to this! But with Albert starting a new school, this is all we need—" Then Mom stopped suddenly and was quiet for a few moments.. "Thank you for telling me," she said slowly. "It is your choice, and I appreciate you giving me the heads up."

Albert knew that his mom had been smiling more lately, and that she seemed to be less angry and ashamed of his father these days, but still . . . he couldn't believe she was okay with his marching in the Pride parade in front of the whole city!

"Thank you so much, Shuchun," his father said. "Four months ago, you wouldn't have reacted that way. I want you to know I appreciate you and your reaction very much."

Mom must have nodded, because a few seconds later, Dad opened up Albert's door.

"Hey, kiddo. We're leaving now. Everything's cool."

Albert shook his head. "Are you sure?" he asked.

"Well, son, you know your mom; sometimes it just takes a little while for her to get used to something. But it'll all work out, I promise."

Albert decided to trust that his dad was right. "Hope so, Dad," he replied. "See you next weekend."

Dad came over and gave Albert a hug, then quickly left his room and their apartment with Guillermo.

Albert turned to the packet he had received from Hunter on Friday, which was sitting on his desk. He hadn't had time to look it over yet, since he had been in Vermont all weekend.

He picked it up and looked at his fall schedule. "Communications and Theater," he read out loud to himself. *Sounds like something my parents should be taking,* he thought.

43

Church camp was all right, but there wasn't much going on.

They didn't even have a pool! Alexa spent her summer days sweating up a storm inside the Harlem church, where she had been going on Sundays with her family since she could remember. She did some cool arts and crafts projects, and they brought in some interesting entertainers every Friday. But it wasn't exactly Alexa's idea of a good time.

"All in the name of making some great connections in our community," her dad had told her. Alexa wasn't so sure it was worth it.

She was super excited to get away on vacation the last week of August. They were going to Saratoga Springs in upstate New York to stay in an air-conditioned cottage on a lake. Alexa packed a different bathing suit for each day and a bunch of books to read (she heard cell phone reception was really bad up by the lake). She also brought the orientation packet she had gotten from

Hunter, which she was excited to devour from cover to cover.

The car ride up there on Friday was uneventful. Alexa took her headphones so she wouldn't have to deal with Celia's "soft rock" junk. The weather was beautiful too: eighty degrees and sunny, without a cloud in the sky.

The problem was the weather once they *arrived* in Saratoga. It rained on Saturday. It rained on Sunday. Then there were thunderstorms on Monday. By the time Alexa had been there for four days, she still hadn't used even one of her bathing suits!

No sun, no swimming, no cell service. By Tuesday night, the three of them were going pretty stir crazy.

"Alexa, why don't you get that orientation packet out from Hunter?" Dad suggested as they sat on the couch after dinner Tuesday evening. "Seems like now would be a great time to go over all that stuff, don't you think?"

"Yeah, you're right," she admitted. "I've almost finished all the books I brought since the rain won't stop." Alexa sprang up and went to her room.

"Now, Alexa, you know I can't do anything about the weather, right?" her dad called after her.

"I know. I'm sorry, Dad. I'm just going crazy here!" Alexa said as she walked back into the living room with her orientation packet. She sat on the floor in front of Dad and Celia and opened the packet on the coffee table in front of her.

"Let's see here . . . my schedule says I'm in homeroom

7-2, whatever that means. I start with math class, then Earth Science, then Spanish."

"Si, si!" said Celia with a Spanish accent.

Alexa laughed. "Yeah, okay, Celia," she said teasingly. "Anyway, then I have something called Communications & Theater. I wonder what that is. Then lunch, then gym, then English, and then history. Pretty decent schedule, I think!"

"Communications and Theater . . . that does sound interesting," Dad agreed. "I don't think I ever took a class like that, in high school *or* college!"

"Hey, I have an idea!" Celia interrupted. "Let's play charades! It'll be just like Communications and Theater."

Alexa looked out the window at the rain, then shrugged. "Okay, Celia," she said. She pointed at Celia. "You go first."

"Okay." Celia smiled, got up, thought for a moment, and started making signals with her hands. Alexa and her dad figured out that it was a movie, with two words. *First word: all over, no, everywhere, no, the world, no, America, yes!*

America, that was it.

Second word: eating, food, delicious food, cookies, no, cake, no, pie, yes!

America and Pie . . .

"*American Pie!*" yelled Dad.

"You got it!" cheered Celia. "That's a favorite of mine from a while back. Have you seen it, Alexa?"

"No, she hasn't seen it, Celia," Dad interjected sternly. "I didn't allow it."

Alexa had asked to see it the year before, and her dad had said no. He had said it wasn't age appropriate, as there was foul language and references to "adult" stuff. "But more importantly," Dad had said, "It's the whitest movie you'll ever see. No Black characters, not even extras."

"We try not to play movies around here that don't have appropriate racial representation," snapped Dad to his quickly-less-enthusiastic wife. Leave it to Celia to choose the whitest movie ever in round one of charades.

"I'm sorry, honey," Celia apologized to Dad. She looked at Alexa like a sad puppy dog who had just been caught sitting on the couch. "I'm an idiot. It just seemed like an easy pick for a round of charades. . . ." She was shaking her head.

Alexa couldn't believe Celia didn't know their representation rule. *I guess that's what happens when you get married after only one year together*, she thought. Her mom and dad had been high school sweethearts. They had known everything about each other. Alexa sighed and looked at Celia. "It's okay," Alexa said. "You meant well. I'm going to go to my room for a while."

The moment she closed the door to her bedroom, Alexa began to cry. She wasn't sure exactly why. She felt overwhelmed by the incident, or maybe it was the fact that she hadn't been swimming or spent more than ten minutes outside in the whole time she'd been away. Maybe she also felt anxious about starting a new school, or maybe it was residual feelings about Celia trying to replace her mom.

Or maybe it was everything.

She needed a vacation from this vacation.

44

David felt like he had been waiting for Hunter's opening day for years. It was his first day at his new school. No more Tony, no more bullies, no more being looked down upon for being smart.

Dad had been in the hospital for three weeks and had come home only a couple of nights before. Things between his parents weren't great, but they weren't awful either. Mom and Dad seemed to be communicating, and Dad was taking his medicine to keep his mood stabilized. That felt reassuring. It meant David could focus on getting ready for his first day instead of worrying about his family.

David was definitely nervous: about starting a new school, not knowing anyone, and the long subway ride to get there. But above all else, he was excited—so excited that he had set his alarm clock for 5:30, but actually woke up at 5:15 a.m. on his own!

David brushed his teeth, showered, and got dressed. He made himself some cereal for breakfast. By 6:15, he was ready to go, super early.

"Mom, Dad! I'm leaving!" David said as he knocked and opened the door to their bedroom.

They shuffled a bit in their bed. Dad was snoring, but Mom looked up. "What time is it?" she asked.

"It's 6:15, but I'm ready to go!" David replied. "I've been up since five. Do you mind if I go now? I want to be early on day one!"

"No, you can go," said Mom through a yawn. "Good luck, I'm proud of you." Then she turned to Dad. "Wake up! David's leaving!" she snarled.

Dad turned over and kept snoring.

"Oh well," Mom said. "Good luck! Text me when you get to school, okay?"

"Okay, Mom," said David. "I'm outta here!"

David went downstairs, put on his Mets jacket, and headed out the door. It was still pretty dark out, and the street was quiet. He headed down the avenue two blocks until he got to the train station. Nearly ninety minutes later (thanks to a train delay), David had arrived at his new school. Good thing he had left early!

The school building was as he remembered it: a big, brick, kind-of-scary building from the outside, but a much friendlier space on the inside. A huge "Welcome back!" poster greeted him when he entered the lobby.

He had to report to room 210 for homeroom, class 7-2, at 8 a.m. It was already 7:45. David saw tons of kids— some a lot older—on his way upstairs. He realized there were kids in high school here, some much older than he

Normal

was. He saw a few faces he recognized from the day he had taken the test. In fact, when David walked into room 210, he immediately saw one of the kids he had been sitting next to for the test.

He went over to sit by her while he tried to think of her name.

"Hi, I'm Tiffany," the cute redhead said, turning to him. "We sat next to each other at the test."

"Yeah, you're right," David said with an awkward smile, sitting down beside her. "Well, congrats on getting in and all."

Tiffany laughed. "Thanks, same to you," she said. She squinted her eyes and tilted her head. "Sorry, what was your name again?"

"Oh, of course, sorry. I'm David," he grinned sheepishly. "Think we'll have all of our classes together?"

"Yup." She twirled one of her red braids. "I think this 'class 7-2' travels together all day. Except for foreign languages, I think. What language are you taking? I'm taking French."

"Moi aussi!" David said in his best French accent. The one good thing about his previous school was that he had started learning French already. "That means 'me too,' by the way."

"Oh, okay." Tiffany smiled. "Well, anyway, nice talking to you."

With that, the bell rang, and David's first day at Hunter began.

187

Homeroom was pretty boring; just a bunch of rules and procedures and attendance. At least the three kids he had met at the test were in his class—Albert, Tiffany, and Alexa. Albert was one of ten Asian kids in the class, and Alexa was—David looked through the whole room— the only Black kid in the class. *That can't be easy*, David thought.

Math class was next, which David was excited for because it was his best subject. Since it was the first class, it was still pretty boring—a lot of rules—but the teacher was cool. Then there was Earth Science, which wasn't David's favorite subject, but the teacher seemed to be fun. David sat next to Tiffany and Albert in both math and science, and then French, which Albert was also taking. French class was going to be super easy, because most of the other kids had never taken French before, and David had been taking it for two years.

Next up was Communications and Theater. This was the class David had been most curious about all summer. He had read one particularly intriguing course review online that said, "This class will change your life. That is all." So as he approached room 233, at the end of a small, dark hallway, David was filled with anticipation, excitement, and a little anxiety. He saw Alexa, so he plopped into a seat right next to her and waited for the bell to ring.

David looked around the room. There were all sorts of motivational and inspirational posters covering every wall. There were bright colors everywhere—mostly orange, lots of orange. On the desk at the front of the room there was a giant calendar with every day marked in a different fluorescent color, lots of paperweights, and an oversized alarm clock. David read the large words on the blackboard behind it: "Welcome to CT. I am Ms. Marsh. Ready? Set? GO!"

Then the bell rang.

45

Tiffany woke up three times the night before her first day at Hunter. She tossed and turned all night. She was so anxious and excited that by the time her alarm clock woke her up at 6:00 a.m., she couldn't quite remember if she'd been having dreams or nightmares.

She was tired from the restless night, but determined not to be late on her first day at a new school. She hopped out of bed, took a shower, brushed her teeth, and put on the clothes she had picked out for herself the night before—a Long Beach sweatshirt she got at the beach over the summer and new jeans her sister had helped her pick out. She was ready to go around 6:30.

Mom, Dad, and Julie were still sleeping, and Tiffany didn't want to bother any of them. She made herself some toast, grabbed an apple and a Vitamin Water, and was out the door a few minutes later.

She had to take an express bus into the city and then transfer to the 6 train. It wasn't an easy ride, but it was easier than the ride she had taken the day of the test, when she'd gotten lost. Tiffany was out of the subway at 96th street by 7:30 and walked toward school in what felt like a sea of kids.

As Tiffany approached the brick building, she felt overwhelmed. It seemed like a thousand kids were all walking into school at the same time. Most of them looked way taller and older than Tiffany. She didn't recognize anyone. Just as she was about to walk into the building, a big kid pushed her to the side and rushed by her. It was a lot to deal with.

She walked into homeroom 7-2 in room 210 and sat in the back. Soon after, a boy she recognized from the test came into the room. Finally, a familiar face! He came and sat by Tiffany. She re-introduced herself and reminded him that she had sat in front of him at the test.

"Yeah, you're right," he answered, stammering a bit. "Well, congrats on getting in and all."

The boy was cute but obviously nervous. She couldn't help but giggle. "Thanks, same to you," she said. She squinted at his face and thought for a moment, but she couldn't remember his name. "Sorry," she said, "what's your name again?"

"Oh, of course, sorry. I'm David," he replied.

They talked about their classes, until he said something Tiffany didn't understand in French, and then the bell rang. But Tiffany decided she liked this familiar face that was warm and smiling. He seemed smart, funny, and nice. Tiffany could definitely deal with that.

The morning classes went pretty well. Math seemed easy enough, and science seemed pretty interesting. French, on the other hand, seemed difficult; the teacher spoke in only French the entire period. Tiffany stuck with David and a couple other kids she recognized from the test—Alexa and Albert—for most of the day. They didn't seem to have much in common, but they all were smart and kind. Tiffany liked that.

Next up was Communications and Theater, or CT, as her homeroom teacher had called it. When Tiffany walked in, she was transported to another world. She immediately noticed the other kids bursting with a silent energy as their heads twisted and turned to take in all the information on the walls. Everywhere she looked, something caught her eye. There was a poster of Supreme Court Justice Ruth Bader Ginsburg, and one of boxer Muhammad Ali with the quote: "Float like a butterfly, sting like a bee! The hands can't hit what the eyes can't see." There were photos on the wall of snow-topped mountain ranges, old cities, islands surrounded by crystal clear blue waters, castles, places Tiffany had never seen before. There was a lot to take in. It was like a funhouse!

Tiffany's eyes landed on a quote from someone she *had* heard of—Dr. Seuss: "Why fit in when you were born to stand out?"

Tiffany liked that, and she liked the classroom a lot.

She was excited to see what this Communication and Theater class was all about.

And then the bell rang.

46

Albert woke up that morning feeling good. He knew how proud his parents were of him, and he was determined to continue to be a success for them.

When his alarm on his phone woke him up at 7:00 a.m., he jumped out of bed. He skipped to the bathroom, took a shower, brushed his teeth, and was dressed by 7:15.

Somehow his mom had him totally beat.

"Albert, I know you don't have a lot of time, but I made you a big breakfast," she called in from the kitchen. "You should not go to school on an empty stomach."

"Thanks, Mom," said Albert as he stumbled into the kitchen with half-tied shoes, "but I've got to run! I don't want to be late on my first day of school."

He looked up and gaped at the kitchen table. His mom had put out quite a spread. There were noodles, wonton, zongzi (Albert's favorite), steamed buns, tea, and more. Plates and bowls filled the table.

Albert looked over at his mom, who was standing next to the table with her head down. "Can you please make me a plate to go, Mom?" he asked. "The food looks great."

"Of course I will," his mom said, now smiling. "It'll take just one minute. Hold on, son." She quickly wrapped up a giant plate of steamed buns, egg pancakes, and red bean paste. She handed Albert the plate and kissed him on the forehead. "I'm so proud of you, my son. Now, eat well and do well."

"Thanks! Bye, Mom," he said and raced out the door to catch the 6 train down the block. It was a quick twenty-minute ride uptown, and Albert tried to guess who else on the train was going to Hunter. That wasn't hard—mostly Chinese kids with large backpacks and headphones were the ones he guessed were going with him. And he was right—most of them got off the train at 96th Street!

Albert recognized several kids from his elementary school on the walk from the train: a couple from his class and a bunch from older classes. He wondered whether this would be the new start he wanted, or if rumors would spread about his secret family shame.

Albert arrived at room 210 a few minutes early. It was a pretty nondescript classroom, with old desks and a whiteboard at the front of the room. He took a seat near the back of the room, next to an African American girl he recognized from the day he took the test. She had a friendly vibe, and Albert already knew one thing about her for sure: she'd have no idea about his dad. So he decided to give it a shot.

"Hi there. I'm Albert," he said to the girl, sticking out his hand to introduce himself.

"I'm Alexa," she replied with a smile, looking relieved. "You ready for this?"

"I think I am," Albert replied. "How about you?"

Alexa shrugged. "I sure hope so. I'm nervous, though."

"I think everybody is, you know?" said Albert, trying to reassure her. "New school and all, traveling all over the city. Where are you from?"

"I'm from the Bronx," she said. "You?"

"Oh, I'm from Chinatown. Pretty quick trip up for me."

"All right, class, let's do this," interrupted their home-room teacher. And Albert's middle school career had begun.

The teacher took attendance and went over some rules, and all the students introduced themselves. Albert recognized David and Tiffany, a couple of kids from the test.

The rest of his morning classes went by pretty fast. Albert sat next to the kids he recognized from the test instead of the kids he knew from his old school. Most of the morning was spent listening to each teacher go over their plans for the year and rules and procedures. The classes didn't seem too tough—except maybe French class, since Albert didn't know any French, and the teacher didn't speak any English!

The classrooms were pretty nondescript until Albert got to room 233. This room was unlike anything Albert had ever seen before: wall-to-wall posters with different motivational sayings and people of all different colors, shapes, and sizes; a desk in the front of the room, overflowing with piles of papers and balancing a giant alarm clock; and a small, thin, older woman sitting at that desk, wearing a gown that made her look more like she should be at museum gala than a classroom.

Albert sat next to Alexa, David, and Tiffany again. The room was abuzz with excitement; students' facial expressions ranged from amusement to shock, and everyone was taking it all in like they were at a circus or an award show or something. Albert figured all his classmates felt like he did: they were in for a different experience than the rest of their classes.

And then the bell rang.

47

Alexa shot up from her bed. She rubbed her temples and looked out her window for a few minutes, thinking about her mother watching over her from Heaven. Celia had pulled back a little from her constant hovering over Alexa since her charades mistake, which was just fine by Alexa. She almost felt bad for Celia . . . almost. Honestly, Alexa was too busy to be worrying about Celia. She was putting all her energy into prepping for her new school.

She had barely left her bed when she smelled fresh bacon cooking from the kitchen. Oh, how she loved bacon! She followed the smell straight to the kitchen, even though she was still in pajamas and hadn't even brushed her teeth yet.

She walked in on a 6:30 a.m. feast.

"Good morning, Alexa!" said her Dad. "Happy first day of school! I've taken the liberty of preparing a few things for breakfast in honor of your first day."

Alexa looked around the kitchen, from the stove to the counter to the table. It was all full: bacon, eggs, pancakes, waffles, grits, fruit salad, and smoothies. It was insane, like Thanksgiving but for breakfast. "Oh my goodness, Dad!" Alexa exclaimed. "How long have you been up?"

"Oh, I've been up for a while. But this is a big day, so it's worth it."

"Good morning," chimed in Celia as she walked into the kitchen. "I followed the smell of bacon and—oh my! Look at all this food!"

"Just breakfast in honor of our Alexa's first day of school at Hunter. Now stop wasting time and sit down before we all make her late!"

They all sat down for the best breakfast Alexa had ever had. It sure beat the cereal her dad had fed her every meal for months after her mom died. Alexa chowed down.

"All right, hope you enjoyed it," Dad said when Alexa finally leaned back and rubbed her belly. "Now go get dressed before you're late for school. Celia's driving you today." Alexa was upset for a second since she'd wanted her dad to drive her into the city for her first day of school. But she was too pumped up to argue.

Alexa ran upstairs and put on her lucky t-shirt, tucking it into her black jeans and new jean jacket. A moment later, she kissed her dad and was out the door. She hopped into Celia's car, and they were off.

There was traffic getting down to the upper east side of Manhattan from the Bronx, but Alexa still managed to arrive a little early for school. She saw hundreds of kids walking to the tall brick building as Celia pulled around the corner to drop her off. It reminded her a lot of the day she had come here to take the test: lots of white kids and Asian kids, but very few Black kids. She felt a lump in her throat and sighed.

"What's the matter?" Celia asked when she put the car in park. Alexa was staring out the window, making no move to get out of the car. Celia tried again. "You a little nervous?"

"No, not really." Alexa turned to Celia. "I just don't see any Black kids, and . . ." Alexa dropped her eyes to look at her hands. "I don't want to be an outcast . . . again."

Celia shook her head and lifted Alexa's chin to face her. "Listen, Alexa. I told you before that you are amazing. Hold your head high. You're going to make great friends here at Hunter—Black, white, or whatever their color. You worked hard to get here, and you're one of the smartest kids in all of New York City. You better turn that frown upside down." Celia beamed her million-dollar smile at Alexa. Alexa couldn't help but smile back. "Now hurry up! You don't want to be late on the first day!"

Alexa looked at Celia, and for the first time, realized that her smile was genuine. Why had she always thought it was fake? Maybe Celia wasn't so bad after all. She seemed to mean well, and she sure tried hard, even if sometimes she tried *too* hard. And Celia *did* make Dad smile a lot.

Alexa went in for a hug. Celia made a small "Oh!" sound, like she was taken by surprise, and it was an awkward hug over the middle console of the car, but it was nice. She said goodbye to Celia, then headed inside the building and up the stairs to room 210.

There were a lot of kids there already, so she sat near the back, where there were still a few empty seats. She looked around and thought she recognized a few kids, but it was hard to tell. There was not another Black person in her whole class. Her stomach dropped and suddenly she felt lonely, the kind of lonely she had felt at her old school, when she sat by herself at lunch.

"Hi there," she heard someone next to her say. She turned to see a boy holding out his hand to her. "I'm Albert," he said.

She smiled and shook his hand. "I'm Alexa," she said. "You ready for this?"

"I think I am," Albert replied. "How about you?"

"I sure hope so. I'm nervous, though." Alexa shrugged.

"I think everybody is, you know?" said Albert. "New school and all, traveling all over the city. Where are you from?"

His kindness made Alexa feel more at ease. "I'm from the Bronx," she said. "You?"

"Oh, I'm from Chinatown. Pretty quick trip up for me."

A moment later, class started. For attendance, the teacher asked everyone to share their names and where they were from. It seemed like most of the kids in her class were from Manhattan, Queens, or Brooklyn. Only one kid was from Staten Island, and nobody else in the whole class was from the Bronx. The teacher explained that the students in this class would be traveling together to different subjects throughout the day, and that they would all have the same classes except when they split for foreign language; most of the class was taking French, but some of the class was taking Spanish.

"I'm in French," whispered Albert to Alexa. "You?"

"Spanish," Alexa replied, her smile dropping.

She sat next to Albert in math and science class. They parted ways when she went to Spanish class, but there, there were actually a few students of color. She sat next to two girls who introduced themselves as Yasmine and Patty—they both were from Brooklyn and had thick Brooklyn accents that Alexa liked. Yasmine had beautiful golden hair and nails to match. Patty reminded her a bit of a girl she knew from her block in the Bronx; tall, tan, and tough with long, curly, black hair. Alexa felt a bit more at home. *Dad will be happy about this*, she thought as she chatted with the girls before class started. It seemed like it would be a good class, as the teacher was really dynamic and fun.

After Spanish, it was on to Communications and Theater class. As Alexa walked to room 233, she thought about how talking about this class with her dad had started the game of charades on their vacation. It had been a strange moment, but Alexa had gotten to see something important: Celia *not* being perfect. Alexa could tell that Celia had meant well, and that she felt bad about messing up.

Alexa thought about how happy Celia made her dad. That was important too. Alexa sighed. She was going to have to admit to herself that she didn't really mind that Celia was sticking around.

When Alexa arrived in room 233, she couldn't believe what she saw. There was a disco ball hanging from the ceiling, and a poster of Martin Luther King, Jr. on the wall. There was every color of the rainbow splashed around the room, from the brightly colored chairs to the walls covered in all types of posters and pictures. It was like a giant playroom for twelve-year-olds! Alexa didn't know what to think. The energy of the room was incredible. It felt like a music concert was about to begin, a sense of excitement and anticipation filling the room.

And then the bell rang.

48

"Welcome, welcome, welcome!" exclaimed the thin, small woman standing in the front of the classroom wearing what seemed to be an evening gown. Her dress was bright red, like the color of the heart in the "I heart NY" t-shirts, and it was big and round, and went all the way down to the floor. It had short sleeves and a high turtleneck, which made the gray and brown curls sticking out all over her head look like a bouquet of flowers. Her dark brown skin glowed underneath golden bracelets that made music when she waved her arms as she spoke. She had high cheekbones, thick eyebrows, and piercing hazel eyes that shined bright every time the shimmery lights from the disco ball hit them. She looked more like a fairy godmother than a teacher.

She walked behind her desk and pointed a piece of chalk toward the writing on the blackboard. She took a visibly large breath and belted out, "My name is Ms. Carol Judy Marsh, and this is Communications and Theater. Please call me Ms. Marsh. My pronouns of choice are 'she' and 'her,' and I am originally from Brooklyn, New York. I am excited for a brand-new round of the most memorable class you will ever experience."

The whole class was mesmerized. This certainly wasn't like the rest of their morning classes.

David turned toward Tiffany and whispered, "Her pronouns means she identifies as a woman."

Tiffany rolled her eyes. "Duh," she whispered back.

Alexa leaned over toward Albert on her right. "I think I like this," she whispered to him. "It's kind of crazy, though."

"Yeah," Albert whispered back and grinned at her. He eagerly turned back toward the front.

"Now, each of you will do what I just did. Please say your full legal name, what name you prefer to be called, and what pronouns you identify with. Then say what borough of this fine city you call home." She turned to write on the board behind her: *legal name, preferred name, preferred pronouns, home borough.* "We'll go around the room, nice and loud, please, beginning with you," she said and pointed to David.

David gulped. He sat up straight and cleared his throat. "Hi. My legal name is actually Charles David Kaplan, but I prefer to be called David. My pronouns are he/him, and I'm from Brooklyn."

"Thank you, David!" Ms. Marsh belted from the front of the room. "Well done, sir. Way to get us started! Not so tough, right? Now, who's next?" She motioned to Tiffany.

"Hi there! I'm Tiffany Molly Russo. I go by Tiffany or Tiff, either is good. My pronouns are she/her, and I'm from Queens."

"Let's keep it going!" Ms. Marsh laughed and did a drumroll with her fingers on her desk. "We're on a roll! Welcome to CT class, as we call it, Tiffany. Next!"

"Hello, I'm Albert. Albert Wang. No middle name. Call me Albert. I'm definitely a he. I'm from Manhattan. Chinatown. How did I do?"

"You did splendidly, Albert! Welcome to CT! And next!" Ms. Marsh motioned to Alexa.

"Hi, I'm Alexa Rose Ellis. I prefer Alexa, thanks. I use she/her pronouns. And I'm from the Bronx. Nice meeting you, Ms. Marsh."

"And nice meeting you, Alexa! Next up!"

Ms. Marsh continued around the room like that, seeming like a larger-than-life fairy of some sort. She motioned to the next person with as much energy as she had the first four, and it proceeded to go: Jason from Queens, then Priscilla from Manhattan, Tait from Brooklyn, and Kevin from Queens. Each student shared their info, and each time, Ms. Marsh greeted them with lots of energy and excitement.

As for the personal pronouns, it seemed like it was the first time most of the kids had had much experience with that sort of language. And each of their "preferred pronouns" was as expected . . . until the very last student of the class, that is.

"Hello, my name is listed as Jacqueline Elizabeth Johnson. I prefer Jackson, and my pronouns are 'he' and 'his.' Yes, I was born female, but I identify as male now, thank you very much for asking, Ms. Marsh. Oh, and I'm from Manhattan."

"Welcome, Jackson, sir," exclaimed Ms. Marsh.

There was a noticeable hush over the classroom at that point. David, Tiffany, Albert, and Alexa all strained to see around each other to look at Jackson again.

"Well then, that's everybody!" said Ms. Marsh. "By now you may have realized that this class is not like other classes. We are going to learn how to speak and to communicate in this class. We are going to learn how to listen. And most of all, if things go as planned here, we are going to learn to love each other for who we are and for our differences."

The class was completely silent. Ms. Marsh looked around the half circle of wide-eyed faces before her and she smiled.

"So, we're just getting started, aren't we?" she said. "Here's your homework assignment: I want you to think about your scariest, most embarrassing family secret. Hopefully, it's something you've never shared with anyone. It should definitely be something that you haven't shared with your new classmates yet, but that's easy; it's the first day!" She chuckled. "Anyway, I want you to write down that family secret in a paragraph. No more than six sentences *max*. And tomorrow, we will all share with the rest of the class. Any questions?"

The class remained silent.

Ms. Marsh sat on the front of her desk and surveyed the class once more. Sounding like a teacher for the first time since class had begun, she stood quickly and said, "I'll assume your silence means you all understand the assignment perfectly, and in that case, I'll see you tomorrow. It'll be a big day for us all. And with that, I bid you adieu in 5-4-3-2-1!"

And there was the bell.

49

David was freaking out. That was the most intense thing he'd ever experienced at school; in fact, if it weren't for his dad's mental illness, it would be the most intense thing he'd ever experienced, period.

Speaking of which, as soon as Ms. Marsh had said "most embarrassing family secret," all David could think about was his dad. He wasn't necessarily embarrassed about his dad; it was just that he *felt* like he should be embarrassed. Or perhaps, he was just confused about whether to be embarrassed or not. In any case, David was obsessing about that crazy class on his way to lunch, which was in the cafeteria with the rest of the school.

"That was *nuts!*" Tiffany's eyes were as wide and bright as her smile when she interrupted David's train of thought as he walked toward the cafeteria. "I mean, what's the deal with her?"

"I don't know." David shook his head. "I read the online reviews on her, so I thought I was prepared. But I wasn't ready for *that!*"

"Seriously, me either." Tiffany's pigtails swung around her shoulders. "Hey, a bunch of kids from our class are going to sit together at lunch. You should join us!"

"Cool, thanks," David said as he puffed out his shoulders to hide his inner sigh of relief. "We can talk about our first morning, and Ms. Marsh. Have you ever seen anything like that?"

"Never. That was crazy!" replied Tiffany. "I mean, that was, like, totally nuts."

David really didn't like the words "crazy" or "nuts." After being through what he'd been through over the past year, he was particularly sensitive to words about mental illness or people with mental illness. But it was the first day at a new school, and he wanted to make a good first impression.

"Yeah, she was crazy!" he said awkwardly.

They walked to a table in the middle of the cafeteria. Albert and Alexa were already there, along with a bunch of other kids whose names he couldn't remember. At first glance, they looked like they were a bunch of misfits that didn't have anything in common with each other. On the other hand, they were all the "smart kids" in their previous schools, just like David had been in the "nerd herd." Here, everyone was in the "nerd herd." So maybe he could fit in.

David was trying to follow the conversation at lunch, but all he could think about was the homework assignment from Ms. Marsh. He'd talked a lot in therapy about his dad's mental illness, but he hadn't ever talked to other

kids about it. He hadn't even told his best friend about it—
how was he supposed to suddenly tell all these new kids
at a new school? What would they think of him and his
messed-up family?

"David!" Tiffany waved her hands in his face. "I called
your name like four times! Anyway, do you know what
you're going to talk about in Ms. Marsh's class tomorrow?"

"Nah, I can't think of anything yet," David lied. "I'm
sure I'll think of something, though. This chocolate milk
is lit!"

"Uh, okay." Tiffany laughed at his awkwardness. "Hey,
what's your Instagram?"

"It's davidkaplan42. Follow me and I'll follow you
back."

"Cool." Tiffany looked at her phone. "Okay, well, we
should finish up lunch and go to our next class, shouldn't
we?"

"Yeah," Albert chimed in. "Let's do this, class 7-2!"

David took a deep breath in and stood up from the
table. "Yup, let's do this!" he said.

Afternoon classes were interesting, but David couldn't
help but think of that assignment from Ms. Marsh. After
the last bell rang, his worry carried into the long train ride
home where he took his first step at answering the assignment and writing his paragraph: "My most embarrassing
family secret is that my dad has bipolar disorder."

That was all he could write.

The hour-plus-long train ride came to an end, and

David collected his things and exited the subway car. He walked up two streets until he got to his Brooklyn brownstone home, wondering as he walked whether either of his parents would be home waiting for him.

His mom met him at the front door. "How was your first day?" she asked, smiling.

David smiled back. "Good," he said.

"So, what happened?" she continued, her gaze following him as he strode by her.

David tried to think of something to tell her, but he could only think of the assignment. "Nothing," he said.

His mom laughed. "Okay!" she said. "Any homework?"

"Nope," David replied. He wanted to be done with the conversation. He wanted to tell her about it, but he just couldn't. He wanted to get upstairs and get it over with.

But as soon as he got to the top of the stairs, David paused. If he had learned anything from Mary, it was to articulate his feelings, calmly but directly. So he turned around and went back down the stairs.

"Mom, actually, you got a minute?" David asked, scratching his face nervously.

She smiled warmly. "Sure, of course."

David took a deep breath in and out. "I have this assignment to write about an embarrassing family secret. But actually, I'm not embarrassed about Dad anymore. Sometimes I get scared, and sometimes I get angry for having to take care of my brother and sister when I'm just a kid myself. But I'm not embarrassed. I just wanted to let you know how I was feeling." He paused and looked up sheepishly.

"Wow, David," Mom answered. She sounded like the wind had been knocked out of her. "I am so sorry that you are having to go through this. You have been so strong; for all of us." She walked over to stand in front of David and took his hands in hers. "I know it might seem like I don't hear you or see you, but I do. I promise. And I love you. I love you so much. And I don't want you to be scared . . ." Mom paused and shook her head. Her eyes filled with tears as she hugged him tightly and continued, "I'm grateful for how mature you are; taking care of so much around the house when I've been busy. Going to therapy. Talking to me. It's just been so hard since your father's diagnosis." She loosened her hug, moved David's hair out of his face, and looked him in the eyes. "Please know I am working hard to try and make life as normal as possible for all of us with all that's going on. And boy oh boy, am I proud of you."

"Thanks, Mom." David said softly.

Suddenly, David felt brave and motivated about the homework. He gave his mom a big hug and raced back up the stairs. He took out that sheet of paper from the train ride and finished his paragraph. Tomorrow, he would have the courage. Tomorrow, he'd give vulnerability a shot. Tomorrow . . . .

It must have been awfully long first day, because by 7:45 p.m., David was fast asleep.

50

It was lunchtime on her first day of school, and Tiffany finally had a chance to check social media. She was relieved to be out of class and checking her phone to see everyone's stories from the day. It wasn't that she wanted to see what was going on with everyone she knew; it was just that, after Ms. Marsh's class, she desperately needed a quick escape from reality.

But then, Tiffany remembered something: she didn't have to look on her phone for an escape—she had made some new friends that day. She turned around to see Alexa walking out of the classroom behind her. "Hey, Alexa! Should we all grab lunch?"

"Sure," Alexa said with a smile. "What was that? He . . . she . . . what?"

"I know, seriously," Tiffany spun around. "I guess we're in for some excitement in that class."

Tiffany was about to walk with a pack of kids to the cafeteria, but she glanced back over her shoulder. She saw David walking through the hall looking pale and kinda sick.

"I'll catch up to you," she said to Alexa, and stopped to wait for David to catch up with her.

As he walked up to her, Tiffany waved. "Hey, David!" she said. "We made it through one morning!" He didn't seem to see her. When he started to walk past her, Tiffany darted up beside him and tried again. "That was nuts!" she said. "I mean, what's the deal with her?"

David's mind seemed to be somewhere else, but she invited him to join the rest of 7-2 in the cafeteria where they could talk about the morning and that class assignment.

They arrived at the cafeteria and immediately smelled the unique smell that only school cafeterias have: a mix of fried food, stale air, and a thousand kids.

Tiffany became the unofficial social chair of the class that first lunch period, directing icebreakers and conversation at the table in a way that made her seem much older than twelve. And it felt good to have the kids look up to her.

Maybe having to be the grown-up in her family would pay off after all.

Afternoon classes went by fast, and before Tiffany knew it, she was heading back home on the express bus. There, after she ran out of stories to check on Instagram and Snapchat, she finally had to think about Ms. Marsh's homework assignment. She knew the obvious thing to write about was her dad's drinking problem, but she also knew her mom and dad preferred to act like he didn't have a problem at all. What if they found out about the paper? What if her dad got in trouble because of it? But she wanted to be truthful. *And anyways,* Tiffany thought, *if I'm so worried about the idea of anyone reading it, doesn't that mean it's exactly the kind of embarrassing family secret Ms. Marsh is asking for?*

Tiffany decided on that bus home to make a bet with herself: if her dad came home at a decent hour that night and stayed sober, she would find something else to write about. If, on the other hand, he came home late and drunk, or came home and got drunk at their house, she would write about his drinking.

The odds didn't feel great.

Tiffany got home at 4:30 and started dinner: a simple chicken and pasta dish. She did her homework for her other classes and caught up on Instagram. Mom got home first at 5:30, followed closely by Julie at 5:45.

Then came the big test. Tiffany wasn't just hoping Dad would come home so she could win the bet; she actually wanted to share her first day at a new school with her family over dinner. But by 6:45, she was already beginning to lose hope. Then the text came from Dad. It was a group text to her and Mom: *Hi ladies. Hope your first day of school went great, Tiffany! Held up for a bit but be home as soon as possible.*

This was a language Tiffany understood far too well. If she'd taken it instead of French, she would get an A easily, because she could translate it right away: *Stopping at the bar. Might be all night.*

"Tiffany, we should have dinner now," her mom called from the kitchen, interrupting Tiffany's thinking and proving her right. "No sense waiting up."

Tiffany took a deep breath, and her chest puffed out as she stormed into the kitchen. "Mom, where is Dad?" she demanded.

Tiffany's mother looked at her with a blank stare. "He's running late, like he sa—"

Tiffany cut her off. "Why are you acting like this is okay?" she asked. Tiffany had reached her breaking point. Her fists were clenched, and her face was as red as strawberries. She was trying not to scream, but she was hurt, and her voice continued to rise. "Why do you keep acting like everything is okay? It's *not okay*! I want to tell Daddy about my first day at school, but he'd rather be at the bar!" She looked down at her hands, and tears started to fall from her eyes. "Daddy's drinking scares me," she admitted. "I don't want him to get hurt. I want him home." She looked up at her mom again. "And I want you to act like you care!" Tiffany yelled.

Her mom stood motionless for a moment, and her eyes filled with tears. She walked over to Tiffany, held her in her arms, and rocked her back and forth.

"I know, Tiff, baby," her mom said quietly in Tiffany's ear. "I know. I'm sorry about how you're feeling about Daddy. I guess I just thought . . . I *hoped* you were oblivious to what was going on." Mom was shaking her head and breathing heavily. "But you're too smart for that, aren't you?" She lifted Tiffany's chin up to look in her eyes. "Honey, I don't want your first day at Hunter to be ruined by your father, okay?" She wiped a tear from Tiffany's cheek. "Dry your eyes and call your sister down for dinner. It'll be a girls' night, all right?"

Over dinner, Tiffany shared the experience of her first day at Hunter with her mom and her sister. She left out the part about Ms. Marsh's class; she didn't want to add any more drama to the night. And she definitely didn't want to give her mom a reason to regret the decision to let her go to school there.

After dinner, with a heavy heart, Tiffany retreated quietly to her room instead of waiting up for her dad. She had read this book so many times, but that night she would write her own ending rather than waiting for it to end like it always did.

Tiffany began to write the assignment for Ms. Marsh: "My dad is an alcoholic."

51

Albert was stunned. He shut his eyes. All summer he had been looking forward to starting over at a new school. All summer he had been excited to put the rumors about his family to rest and begin a new life for himself in a place where nobody knew his secret. And now, on the first day at that new school, he was being asked to share that secret in front of the entire class.

It was unfair. He refused to believe it was happening— maybe if he ignored it, it would go away. Albert suddenly had a quick and simple solution: make something up. Yeah, maybe he would try that on for size. But first, lunch.

It seemed like everybody from his class was sitting together at lunch, so he joined them. Tiffany was already the ringleader, and she seemed a little annoying but well-meaning. The cafeteria looked and smelled and sounded . . . well, like a school cafeteria. It was loud, but it felt like the kids had something in common now, having gone through Ms. Marsh's class . . . even if Albert was afraid to talk about it.

Albert was scanning the room when he locked eyes with Alexa. "What's the Bronx like?" he asked her.

Alexa finished chewing and replied, "I don't know, it's just the Bronx! But there are a lot more Black people in the Bronx than here. That's for sure!" She smiled at Albert. "So, what's it like living in Chinatown?" She took a big bite of her sandwich and waited for his answer.

"I don't know," Albert shrugged. "Pretty cool, I guess. Except you can't find any decent Chinese food anywhere." Albert smirked.

Alexa laughed so hard she almost lost the bite of her sandwich. Albert felt good to have successfully cracked a joke. He tried to have fun the rest of lunch, but his mind kept racing back to his secret and whether he would have to share it or not.

The end of the school day couldn't come fast enough for Albert. As soon as the last bell rang, he texted Paul: *We need to talk. When can you FT?*

On my way home. Give me thirty minutes, Paul replied.

Paul was at the public middle school with all of the kids from his class who hadn't gotten into Hunter. Right about now, Albert was thinking it might have been better if he had gone there with his best friend, instead of agonizing over this crazy new teacher at this crazy new school.

Albert took the 6 train home and settled into his room. The FaceTime from Paul came right on time: "Dude, what's up? How was your first day at Hunter?"

He was dressed a bit more maturely than the Paul he had known, with a collared shirt on. Guess he was growing up too.

"It was pretty good. How was yours?"

Paul shrugged. "All right, no big deal. Mostly the same kids as before. New teachers, and going class to class is pretty cool. How are your teachers, bro?"

"Okay, that's the thing." Albert paused and shook his head. "So I have this class called Communications and Theater, and the teacher, Ms. Marsh, is totally crazy. You'll never guess what my first homework assignment is!"

Paul laughed. "How bad could it be, man? What, does she want you to write some long-ass essay or something?"

"Nope, it's only a paragraph."

"Okay, then it sounds easy, so . . .?"

Albert took in a deep breath. "We are supposed to write about our most embarrassing family secret, Paul. I think you know what that is."

"Whoa! Are you serious? That *is* crazy! Dude, I'm so sorry. Wow. That didn't take long. What's your plan?"

"I don't know, man! That's why I wanted to talk to you. What do you think I should do?"

"Come on, man, you know me—my cousin and everything. Gay people are everywhere. It's not a big deal anymore. Plus, it's not all Chinese kids like at our old school, right?"

"Well, not *all*. But a lot of Asian kids still, yeah. I just can't believe it. This was supposed to be a new school, new opportunity, you know?"

"I know, Albert. But here's the thing: Maybe it still *is* a new opportunity . . . to be yourself—your funny, cool-ass self. And a chance to be honest about your family from the beginning. Maybe it'll be okay to talk about it."

"Yeah, I know. I guess I knew what you'd say. Thanks, brother."

"No problem, bro. Got to go. Later, man."

Albert hung up feeling better. He knew how happy his mom was about him getting into Hunter, and he knew she wouldn't want him to talk about his dad to even a single person, much less his entire class. But he knew his father would want him to talk about it, and more importantly, now he knew what he needed to do for *himself.* It wasn't always about what his mom wanted, anyway. It was about accepting reality and embracing his family for who they were. So Albert got out a notebook and a pen, and began to write his paragraph.

52

Wow, thought Alexa as she walked out of room 233. *What an awesome class! This school certainly is different.*

The whole class was abuzz about the assignment. Alexa wasn't as overwhelmed by the assignment as she was by the whole experience of a school so different from her elementary school. First, instead of everyone being Black, barely anyone was Black. Then it turned out there was a transgender kid in her grade. And she also had a teacher who either wanted to embarrass the whole class or make them cry. She wasn't sure.

"Hey, Alexa! Should we grab lunch?" Tiffany asked as they walked out of the classroom and into the hallway.

"Sure!" Alexa smiled. "What *was* that?" she asked, nodding her head at room 233. "He . . . she . . . what?"

They talked for second, then Tiffany peeled off to talk to that kid David and told Alexa she'd meet her in the cafeteria. But as Alexa walked down the hallway with the rest of the class, she wasn't quite so sure. She walked into the smelly cafeteria and surveyed the landscape. Yes, it was a lot whiter and more Asian than her previous school. But she spotted some Black kids too, some of whom were sitting together at one table. Alexa found herself with a new problem she hadn't expected: sit with the Black kids or sit with her traveling class?

She knew how important it was to her dad for her to make friends with other Black kids. But she also wanted to bond with the kids in her new class, and it was only the first day. There was no rush. It would be really nice to actually have friends in her class for a change. Alexa decided to stay and hang with Tiffany and the crew.

Everyone was talking about the homework assignment from Communications and Theater over lunch, even the kids who had a different CT teacher. Alexa wasn't sure what she was going to write about. She definitely wasn't embarrassed that her mom had died of cancer, and it definitely wasn't a secret, even though it was an important part of her family experience. She was kind of embarrassed about her dad remarrying a white woman, but that wasn't a family secret either. And would Celia's feelings be hurt if she found out that's what Alexa had written about?

Alexa looked up and met Albert's eyes.

"What's the Bronx like?" he asked her.

Alexa finished chewing and replied, "I don't know, it's just the Bronx! But there are a lot more Black people in the Bronx than here. That's for sure!" She smiled to let him know it was okay. "So, what's it like living in Chinatown?" Alexa took a bite of her sandwich and leaned in to hear him.

"I don't know," Albert shrugged. "Pretty cool, I guess. Except you can't find any decent Chinese food anywhere."

Alexa laughed *hard*. So hard that she almost spit out her sandwich. She had never really known an Asian kid before, but she already knew she liked this boy.

After lunch, Alexa went to the rest of her classes. Compared to Ms. Marsh, every teacher and class seemed kind of lame. But that also felt like a much-needed break, and she had found a little first-day friend group in Tiffany, Albert, and David that seemed random but pretty cool.

While most kids were taking the subway or a bus home (and the plan was for Alexa to do that beginning on the second day of school), Alexa's dad picked her up. She was grateful when she saw his car pulling up to the curb outside school.

"Hi there, middle schooler!" her dorky-as-ever dad shouted as she climbed into the passenger seat of the car. "How was your first day of school?"

"Pretty good," Alexa said.

He rolled his eyes. "Okay, tell me more," he prodded. "Don't make me pull teeth to get this out of you. I need info! Teachers, kids—I want to know everything!"

"Okay, okay," Alexa said with a smile. "The kids are pretty cool. They are definitely very different from my old school. Classes are awesome. Everyone knew the answers in math class! *Everyone*! It was funny. And I have this one teacher, Ms. Marsh. She was wearing a party dress and she has a disco ball hanging from the ceiling and . . ." Alexa paused to catch her breath.

Dad raised his eyebrows. "Wow, sounds like quite a day." He leaned his shoulder into hers. "Okay, so—"

"I know. Calm down, Dad," interrupted Alexa. "I'll tell you everything that happened today. Stat!"

Dad nodded, chuckled, and turned to her for a moment before looking back at the road ahead. Alexa took a deep breath before she began. "Okay, so, all in all, it was pretty cool . . . and also a lot. There's a high school too, so there's lots of kids, all new faces. Everywhere. My main class, 7-2—there are twenty-five of us, and I'm the only Black kid in that class. But to be honest, it wasn't bad. I did meet a couple of cool Latina girls in my Spanish class. I think one of the girls, Patty, said she's Puerto Rican, but we didn't really talk about that, because we were busy talking about science! Everyone is really nice, and that was amazing. I had math, Earth Science, history class . . ."

Dad sighed, then clicked his tongue. "Okay," he said. "How was lunch?"

"I sat with the kids from my traveling class since I had met a few of the kids on the day of the test and we just clicked. It was fun. There was a lot going on, but there are a bunch of Black kids from what looked like different grades sitting together at a table. They all smiled at me when I passed by, which was cool. There were kids from the base-ball team at a table next to us, and you can go outside to the giant courtyard too! It was almost too much. I never thought school could be so . . . I don't know. So awesome!"

Dad smiled. "I'm proud of you, sweetie. And I'm sure you know who else is proud of you today."

"Mom?"

"Well, yes, of course. I'm sure she's smiling down on you right now." Her dad reached over and squeezed Alexa's hand. He continued, "But you know who is really excited about your first day of school? Celia. She's been bothering me about you all day. Pick up my phone and see for yourself. Look at the last texts from her while I was waiting for you in the car. She's funny."

Alexa picked up Dad's phone and scrolled through his last few text messages with Celia.

Celia: *How did it go?*

Dad: *She's not out yet, darling. And we'll be home soon.*

Celia: *I know, I know. I'm just so excited! Alexa's first day at the new school* 😚

Dad: *Calm down!* 😄 *She's outside now talking to a kid in a Mets jacket. The Mets are the best!*

Celia: *Don't start with that!* 😠

Dad: *Here she comes.*

Celia: *I'm on my way home. I hope she had the best day! I can't wait to hear all about it.*

Alexa smiled. It felt pretty nice to read Celia's messages about her.

"Thank you, Dad," she said. "Can we listen to music for the rest of the trip home?"

"Sure thing," he said, and turned on the radio.

Alexa closed her eyes as Hot 97 played pop song after pop song, and she thought about her assignment for Ms. Marsh.

Now she knew what she was going to write about when she got home.

53

"You're all here! That's a great sign!" Ms. Marsh exclaimed as she began class on the second day of school. "I didn't scare any of you young people away, I guess." There was a nervous energy jumping around the room. People were struggling to make eye contact with one another, not knowing what anybody would be sharing in just a few moments.

Ms. Marsh sat on the edge of her desk. "I promise you will get through today, and you will all be okay. Now, we have a lot to cover in forty-nine minutes, so let's begin."

She got up, walked toward the board, and then spun back around to face the class again. "First, I'd like to do a quick anonymous survey, okay? Everybody take out a sheet of paper and make two boxes, one marked 'yes' and one marked 'no.'" She paused as students ruffled their papers and followed her instructions. "Now, write the following question above those boxes: Is my family 'normal'?" She used air quotes when she said "normal."

Ms. Marsh continued, "Then, check the box that fits

your family, fold the paper, and send it to the front of the room where I will collect them all. Go ahead now!"

David, Tiffany, Albert, and Alexa had sat together, and they followed her instructions along with the rest of class. They had been sitting together in all their classes that morning and were becoming fast friends: a Jewish boy, an Italian girl, a Chinese boy, and an African-American girl—perhaps not a typical middle school friend group, but this was not a typical middle school.

"All right, then!" Ms. Marsh exclaimed a few minutes later. "Thanks for acting fast. I've just tallied the results—trust me, it was easy—and here are the grand totals." She began to write the words on the board at the front of the room as she spoke them out loud: "Is my family normal? YES: 0. No: 25."

The twenty-five students looked on as Ms. Marsh walked around the room slowly. "This is my twentieth year of teaching, and today makes 501 'no' votes against three 'yes' votes total. Five-hundred and one to three. So, if nobody's family is normal, I guess we're all abnormal, eh? Or maybe being normal isn't so important?" She paused and looked around the hushed room. "I'll tell you what," she continued, "the data doesn't lie, but people's stories are even more powerful. So please take out your home-work assignments from yesterday, your paragraphs."

There was a sudden sound of shuffling of papers as everyone took out their homework assignment, but there was barely a whisper in the room. Everyone was looking around, up and down, anywhere but at each other, and definitely not at Ms. Marsh. Everyone seemed scared they would have to read their paragraph out loud first.

"Okay, some quick ground rules before we get started," Ms. Marsh announced. "We will go from right to left, meaning Jackson, you're up first, and Alexa, you'll go last. Everyone will have up to sixty seconds to share what you've written—no more, no less. Sixty seconds is more than enough time. And one more thing: the confidentiality oath. All phones away, and everyone raise your right hand and repeat after me."

David turned to Tiffany and Alexa, and Alexa turned to Albert. The four of them raised their right hands along with the rest of the class and repeated these words after their teacher: "I do hereby promise that what is said in Ms. Marsh's class stays in Ms. Marsh's class, period, end of story. Our confidentiality is sacred. Confidentiality breeds trust, and trust is everything."

The class put their hands down, and Ms. Marsh turned to Jackson. "One minute on the clock. Jackson, please stand and read. On your mark, get set, go!"

Jackson stood up and read what he had written: "I'm not embarrassed at all that I'm transgender. But my family secret is how my parents reacted. My mom was upset at first when I came out to her, but now she's okay. It's been two years, but my dad has never really gotten used to it. And that makes me sad. I'm the same person I've always been, I just feel unloved by my parents sometimes."

Jackson's eyes teared up a little as he spoke, and a wave of empathy covered the room. There wasn't much time for small talk or consolation, though.

"Thank you so much, Jackson," Ms. Marsh said. "Kevin, you're up next."

Kevin, a long-haired, short Korean boy, stood up and said, "My dad left when I was very young. My mom has raised me from the start, working two jobs to make sure my brother and me have what we need. I've never heard from my dad, who abandoned me."

"Thank you for sharing, Kevin," said Ms. Marsh. "Next up, Samantha."

Samantha got up and talked about her older sister's drug addiction. Then, one by one, each student in the class talked about issues and challenges that made them feel like their family wasn't normal: substance abuse, abandonment, death, divorce, infidelity, crimes, siblings with special needs, parents losing jobs, and being poor, to name a few. Their voices were powerful and strong, even at times in sadness, fear, and embarrassment. There were four students left to go.

"Thank you, Laura. Next up: David."

The good news for David was that by the time twenty-one students had gone, it was much easier to be brave. But even still, he was terrified. David stood up, cleared his throat, and began to read: "My most embarrassing family secret is that my dad has bipolar disorder. It's a psych illness where you're either really sad or really happy. But when he's manic, it can be dangerous. So he's been hospitalized four times in the last year. It's been really hard on my mom and my brother and sister and me. Therapy has helped me a lot."

David sat down with tears in his eyes. He hadn't wanted to cry, but as he finished speaking, he felt a wave of emotion: relief. Tiffany gave him a small smile and reached out her hand to grab ahold of David's. His secret was out, and his friends still liked him. He felt better already.

"Thank you, David. Tiffany, you're up next."

Tiffany stood up and said these words out loud for the first time in her life: "My dad is an alcoholic. I don't know for sure, but it feels like he drinks every night, and a lot. My mom makes excuses for him, and I help out a lot around the house. But I wish he didn't drink so much."

Tiffany took a big sigh as she sat back down. She'd never experienced a class like this—every student was paying attention, nobody was laughing or snickering or whispering, and it just felt like everybody cared about her. It felt good.

"Thank you, Tiffany. Albert, you're up!"

Albert shot up. He was terrified, so much so that he could feel himself physically shaking, but he was in a hurry to get it over with, having waited in fear for most of the class period. When he read, he spoke fast: "My dad is gay. He came out and left my mom and now he has a boyfriend. This would be a big deal, I think, in any family, but in a Chinese family, it's a huge deal." He looked up from his paper. "My mom really wanted to keep this all a secret, but, well, I guess it's out now."

Albert shot back down as fast as he had risen. He stared down at his desk and couldn't manage to look at his friends. Then Tiffany on his left and Alexa on his right simultaneously whispered to him, "It's okay, Albert." He turned to each of them and smiled.

"Thank you, Albert!" said Ms. Marsh. "Last but not least: Alexa! You're up."

Alexa stood up and looked around the room. She had her paper in front of her, but she decided to break the rules and speak, instead of just reading. "At first I was going to write about my mom dying of cancer. I'm sad about that, but it's not a family secret or anything. And then I was going to write about my dad remarrying a white lady. That's more of an embarrassment to some people, that's for sure. But then I decided, well, I'm not really embarrassed by that. I'm embarrassed that I haven't given my stepmom, Celia, a chance. Sometimes I hate her even though she's trying really hard. That's all I've got."

"Students," rang out Ms. Marsh. "That's all of you. Wowzah! You all did an amazing job. I am so proud. This is a very risky activity, but I felt you could all step up, and you did. When I was a freshman in college, I had a professor who did this activity with us, and it changed my life forever. Made me want to teach. Now, we'll unpack this all a lot more tomorrow, but I've got two things to tell you and one thing for you all to write down first, so take those notebooks and pens back out."

David, Tiffany, Albert, Alexa, and the rest of the class were emotionally spent, but they got out their notebooks as Ms. Marsh continued, "First, a reminder to use confidentiality and have empathy for each other. Everyone has shared something deeply personal today, so please have the tremendous respect for each other that you all deserve. Second, I started class by asking you how many of you felt like your families are normal. Now that you've heard each other's stories, I'll ask you to think over the weekend about how important it really is to be 'normal,' or to come from a 'normal' family. And finally, I'd like you all to write the following definition of 'normal,' my least favorite word in the English language. Are you ready? Go ahead and write this down, the best definition you'll ever hear for the word 'normal.'"

The class looked up in anticipation, and Ms. Marsh paused, looked down at the clock on her desk, and then back up at them when she was ready.

"Normal. N.O.R.M.A.L. Normal is a setting on the washing machine. And that. Is. It!'"

Ms. Marsh, amongst other things, had amazing timing. Three seconds later, the bell rang.

54

That day in Ms. Marsh's classroom changed everything for David, Alexa, Albert, and Tiffany. Of course, they still had their challenges to deal with at home. None of those were going away anytime soon. But for the first time in each of their lives, they didn't feel so alone. They didn't feel like they had to hide from their truths. Most importantly, they didn't feel like their experiences were so abnormal anymore.

In Ms. Marsh's classes after that, they started doing skits and role plays about their greatest fears and where they came from. It was a class that challenged them deeply, helped them to grow into young adults, and helped them form special relationships with one another. And then, each time, just as they were beginning to fall back into their comfort zones, Ms. Marsh would challenge them again to go even deeper, develop more empathy, listen better, be more grateful, speak up, speak out, and speak their truths.

Albert, Alexa, David, and Tiffany continued to be a

tight knit group. Of course, over the next few years, they would all make many more friends and grow in their own ways: David joined the Mathletes (a much more popular group at Hunter than at his previous school) and competed in math competitions across the entire country; Tiffany became a cheerleader, something she never thought possible at her previous school, and something that made her mom super proud; Albert got involved with student government and the school newspaper; and Alexa joined and eventually became vice president of the African American Students Alliance (AASA).

But those first two days of school and Ms. Marsh's class had created an instant bond among the four of them, a bond that would never break. They maintained a group text (aptly named "The Normal 4") throughout middle and high school. Even over the winter holidays, as they spent time with their families, they thought of each other.

Tiffany: *Merry Xmas, my abnormal brothers and sister!*

Albert: *Yah, Merry Christmas. And David, enjoy your Chinese food.*

David: *Haha thanks. Merry Christmas and enjoy the time with your abnormal families.*

Alexa: *You too. Love you all.*

Tiffany: ♥

Albert: 🎄

David: ☺ 👍

Alexa: ♥ ♥ ♥ ♥

Acknowledgements

There are so many people who help to make a book a reality, and I am grateful for all of you, even those whose names don't fit on this page.

First and foremost, I'm grateful to Lindsay Brockington, my coauthor. Lindsay, you brought depth and love to our characters, and your beautiful spirit and words to our pages. Thank you!

Thank you to my family, forever my inspiration. Carrie, I love you today and always. Charlotte and Kate, without your asking for it, this book surely wouldn't exist. Seth, I'm excited for you to be old enough to read this soon!

To Robert, Christina, and our publishing team at Brandylane, thanks for taking a chance on us. Thanks Mary Crook for your tireless efforts, and to the designers and editors and all who contributed. It takes a village!

To Lee Constantine and the team at Publishizer, thanks for validating the concept and helping me presell loads of books.

To all my friends and readers who pre-bought books, thanks for believing in me, and thanks for your epic patience!

—Dave

Dave Kerpen, thank you for the opportunity to write this beautiful book with you. I am forever grateful. Here's to the next chapter.

Mary Crook, thank you for teaching me how to better show the world, the world.

To my mother and stepfather, Linda Brockington and Gé van den Heiligenberg, merci pour tout.

To my sister, Jodi Brockington; Saskia Thompson; Shannon K. Liston; Shelly Aufray, and to all of you who love and support me around the world: "Let we go!"

—Lindsay

About the Authors

DAVE KERPEN is is a *New York Times* bestselling author of three books and a serial entrepreneur. His latest company is Apprentice (ChooseApprentice.com).

Dave has been named one of *Entrepreneur*'s top ten up-and-coming leaders and has been featured on CNBC's *On the Money*, ABC's *World News Tonight*, CBS's *Early Show*, *The New York Times*, and the BBC. He's keynoted at dozens of conferences across the globe including Singapore, Athens, Dubai, San Francisco, and Mexico City.

Dave is the father of three beautiful kids (Charlotte, Kate, and Seth), the husband to an amazing business partner, Carrie Kerpen, and friend to many. You can find out more about him at his website DaveKerpen.com and on social media @DaveKerpen.

LINDSAY BROCKINGTON is a singer, songwriter, band leader, producer, television show host, and photographer. After living in the Caribbean, France, and Australia, Lindsay recently returned home to the Upper West Side to work on her creative projects.

You can listen to Lindsay's music and watch her videos on Spotify, YouTube, Apple Music, Tidal, and Google Play, and on her website lindsaybrockington.com.

CPSIA information can be obtained
at www.ICGtesting.com
Printed in the USA
BVHW031329110322
630955BV00002B/10

9 781953 021632